Khartoum

a novel

Khartoum

a novel

Luke Dixon

Matador
5 Weir Road
Kibworth Beauchamp
Leicester LE8 0LQ, UK
Tel: (+44) 116 279 2299
Fax: (+44) 116 279 2277
Email: books@troubador.co.uk
Web: www.troubador.co.uk/matador

ISBN 978 1848762 367

British Library Cataloguing in Publication Data.
A catalogue record for this book is available from the British Library.

Typeset in 11pt Book Antiqua by Troubador Publishing Ltd, Leicester, UK

Matador is an imprint of Troubador Publishing Ltd

Printed in Great Britain by the MPG Books Group, Bodmin and King's Lynn

For Siobhánn

"I am a part of all that I have met;
Yet all experience is an arch wherethrough
Gleams that untravelled world, whose margin fades
For ever and for ever when I move."

- Tennyson

CHAPTER ONE

Kent And London

He was in the nursery when the call came. The spring sun was playing through the greenhouse and he was teasing at the sprouting seeds. The more robust would be ready for planting out in a couple of weeks when the sun was stronger and spring was here to stay. It was his favourite time of year – new beginnings after the hard weeks of February and March when it had seemed as if the days would be perpetually cold and grey.

'It's the Club, Sir. On the telephone.' Alec Harvey looked up from his seedlings and saw Albert Godby standing by the greenhouse door in his blue overalls, telephone in one hand watering can in the other. 'I said you were busy, but the Secretary was very insistent.' Alec sighed; it could only be trouble. He had not heard anything from the Club in months and had not worked for them for a couple of years or more. Life for him now was his cuttings and his seeds deep in the Kent countryside, not adventures overseas. Foreign travels had become a thing of the past and that was where he had hoped to keep them. 'I'd better talk to them, Albert,' he said wiping the soil from his hands onto his brown corduroy trousers.

The old man handed him the phone and withdrew

discretely. The voice on the end of the telephone was apologetic.

'Sorry to trouble you Alec, especially on a Saturday, but we've a spot of bother in Africa. We thought you might be the man to sort it out.' He recognised the voice, though he had never seen a face to put to it. It was indeed the Club. The seedlings would have to wait; it seemed that he was needed far away.

'What sought of bother?'

'You'd better come up to town to talk about it. It's a little delicate for the telephone. Oh, and bring your passport and your Arab kit. It's going to be hot where you're going. You should be able to catch the three o'clock from Dover. We've arranged for it to make an unscheduled stop at Headcorn for you. You're booked on a flight out on Sunday evening. You can spend tonight at the Club, there will be someone in the bar later to fill you in. Good luck, you'll need it.'

'Thanks,' Alec said but the phone had already gone dead. As he walked back to the house he wondered exactly where he would be going and just how hot it would be.

'Run me a bath,' he called to Albert as he pulled off his boots. 'And plenty of Irish tea in it, I need one of your instant tans.' He need not have asked. Albert Godby had returned from the nursery as Alec was taking the call and was already making preparations for his employer's departure. There was a very large glass of carrot juice waiting for him on a table in the study with a jug of the bright orange liquid beside it. He could hear the sound of a bath being drawn, no doubt full of the tea which would mark the enamel of the ancient tub just as it was meant to darken his skin. Tea and carrot juice; those and his gleaming white Arab *jellabiya* were all the disguise he had ever needed on his adventures in the Middle East and North Africa. He already sported a moustache and had not shaved for a few days, being too engrossed in his tasks in the greenhouse sorting seeds to be sent to regular clients around the country. A good thing too. Another couple of days of growth and his beard would merge with his moustache and convince anyone who did not look too closely that he was a son of Araby rather than a child of the English shires. He would be able to disappear into the dust of wherever he was being sent with no-one noticing his presence. A crumpled linen suit would complement his scruffiness should he have to turn up at some Embassy or a British Council office in western garb. He knew from experience to be prepared for anything.

'Not off to deal with dodgy Arabs again are we, Sir?' asked Godby as he neatly packed the battered canvas suitcase that had been Alec's constant companion in years of travelling.

'Not so much of the dodgy, Albert. They're no dodgier than you and me.'

'That's as maybe, Sir, but they're different, don't forget that. You may be able to pass for one if no-one peers too closely, but remember how different they are or you'll get yourself into one of your scrapes.'

Whatever else he could say about Albert, Alec never doubted either his personal loyalty or his fierce distrust of 'abroad', as he called it. The all purpose factotum who looked after the house and helped in the nursery, Albert had the deepest suspicion of 'the other' in all its many forms, a distrust bred through the generations of a family whose lifetimes had all been spent in the little East Kent village. Now in his sixties, Albert Godby had been a part of Alec's life ever since he could remember. He had probably been in the house when he came back to it as a new born baby forty-five years ago. Alec doubted whether Albert had ever left the village or the estate except for his weekly trip to Ashford for the market.

'I'll be up in London tonight Albert, just as soon as I'm dressed and packed. They've arranged for the train to stop for me.'

'Will you be gone for long?' Albert seemed concerned, not liking anything that upset the regularity and order of life at the house and not wanting to see his employer getting into any more 'scrapes'.

'Difficult to say, but I should think I'll only be away a few days if all goes well.'

'Is there much to be done while you're gone, Sir?'

'Just keep an eye on the strelitzias will you Albert? They should germinate any day now if we're lucky.' The exotic African bird of paradise plants were Alec's proudest achievement, not many others were growing them in England and he had a ready market for as many as he could produce. 'Keep them warm and make sure they don't dry out. Otherwise things should look after themselves.'

Albert disappeared upstairs and Alec heard him turning off the taps on the bath, the old boiler spluttering after the effort of filling the vast enamel tub that had been in the house for a hundred years or more. He was never exactly pale but after a long English winter hidden away in the family pile with only his books and plants for company, Alec looked much more the *kawaja*, the white man, than he usually did. Tea leaves would be infusing his bath with the deep colour of Assam, ready to soak into his skin and disguise the Englishness of his body, ready for it to do whatever was required of it in Africa. He looked into the long mirror standing in the corner of the room as he stepped into the bath. His body was taught and rugged from the daily work in the gardens, his penis neatly circumcised and his hair curly enough to help him pass in the Arab world even stark naked. With the tea stain and carrot juice to darken his skin he would soon look just the part, whatever part that might need to be.

He enjoyed the soak, watching the steam condense and dribble down the windows, wondering where he was be sent that weekend, and trying to remember his Arabic. His heart sighed at the thought of again leaving England and the quiet life he had built for himself in the past few years. His little specialist seed business made just about enough money to pay for the upkeep of the old family home now that he was the only family left to look after it. He was still in his forties but felt as if he had already retired to the quieter type of life that most men never succumbed to for another twenty years. Something though was stirring inside him, for despite the comforts of home and the misty beauty of the Kent countryside, a part of him was never truly able to resist the lure of travel and the challenge of adventures overseas. Even now, after so many years of jaunting to the remotest corners of the globe, there were still things to see, places to go. He felt no allegiance to his country, certainly not to the government that was currently running it with their misbegotten foreign policies, but he did think of himself as English and he did love his home and his neighbours and friends and the life and values that they stood for. For him the Club represented those values writ large and if the Secretary of the Club said it was important and he was needed then this would not be a task he could easily refuse.

Albert had left him a warm towel and replenished the glass of carrot juice to add to the darkness of his skin. A few more of those over the next twenty four hours and he would be as orange under the tea stains as a chat show host on the daytime television that gave Albert his particular take on the world outside. He dried himself on the vast, threadbare towel that had been in the house for years and took the *jellabiya* out from the bottom draw of the chest in his bedroom. It was the lightest, thinnest and yet most capacious of garments, a swathe of pure white cotton that almost reached to the floor and with sleeves that he could lose his hands in. It had been a long while since he had worn it, not since that business in the Yemen. Albert had not only got the blood stains out, but patched up the bullet hole. He had had it for years and as he put it on remembered having bought it as a student in the *souk* in Cairo, the merchants chattering and laughing as he had struggled to put in on. He had taken an instant liking for it as soon as he saw it hanging inside the stall. Alec always enjoyed dressing up and the long Arab gown was something he had always wanted to wear. It was on that first trip to Cairo visiting his Uncle Leo as a young man trying to improve his Arabic that he decided to buy one. After a while the shopkeeper had taken pity on him and shown how it was possible to slide inside it with the ease of one graceful movement, ruching it above his head and letting it drop down in what seemed to him a magical transformation. There was a hat to go with it with a subtle trace of silk embroidery, neatly folded in the pocket, and he put that on too. As he caught sight of himself in the wardrobe mirror, his body felt at ease in this disguise, a different sort of ease from the comfort he felt when he was in his boots in the greenhouses. For a moment he wondered whether the boots or the *jellabiya* were the true disguise.

He would need to polish up his Arabic. Not that it would

take much to bring it all back. Trying to recollect it as he had lain in the bath had made him realise just how much he had missed speaking it, though days could go by at home when he did not even speak any English, save for the occasional word or two to Albert. He had struggled with languages at school and could barely stutter through his French and German oral examinations. His old school masters would have been very surprised indeed to learn that he had grown up to spend so much time in other countries speaking a foreign language like a native. Arabic had delighted him from the first moment he had heard it on that glorious summer between school and University with his Uncle Leo who was working as a cultural attaché at the British Embassy in Cairo. He found himself speaking it from the moment he got off the plane and it came to him as the most natural of skills, just as years struggling with European languages at school had been unnatural. Speaking it was one thing, reading and writing quite another. But he had persevered and could make out most of what he needed to read and could even write the odd bit of script if he had too. Now on a chilly afternoon forty miles outside of London it did not seem peculiar at all to be walking around his bedroom collecting things for his trip and speaking to himself in Arabic as he did so. He had no doubt that it would all come back to him when he needed it and probably even before if he could find an Arab to talk to before he left. Spending some of the weekend brushing up his language skills in London before he had to leave would be fun. There was that little Moroccan restaurant he used to frequent in Soho with its all-night subterranean bar. He would while away an hour or two there before his flight.

The train to London was as grubby and slow as ever, a tawdry Third World service through the Garden of England. It did at least make the unscheduled stop at Headcorn that he had been promised. He waved farewell to Albert, who had waited until he had climbed aboard before turning around the mud splattered Land Rover and returning across the level crossing, and lost himself in the day's papers that he had picked up from the village shop on their way to the station. Nothing on any of the foreign pages gave much of a clue as to what was happening in Africa. There were disputed elections in Kenya and that was the only African news in any of the papers. It seemed that the British media could only cover one story from the 'dark continent' at a time.

An hour later he was at Charing Cross Station where he came through the barriers to see a crowd of humanity looking up at the departure boards, eyes fixed upwards waiting for news of a train that would take them away from the city. Alec pushed through the crowd, a single figure elbowing himself in the opposite direction to everyone else and jumped into a taxi for the short ride to the Club. It was a beautiful afternoon; the sunlight glinted on Landseer's lions as they went around Trafalgar Square, turned along Pall Mall and into a little road behind the Ritz Hotel. The clocks had just gone forward and the late afternoons were extending into early evenings just warm enough for *al fresco* drinks. Outside the pubs, young people laughed and flirted over glasses of wine, and middle-aged men sank solitary pints of lager.

'CONTINENTAL HOUSE World Headquarters of the Royal Continental Club' said the brass plaque on the gates of an imposing building set back discretely from a road that was going nowhere, a *cul-de-sac* between Mayfair and Green Park. Alec paid off the cabbie and pushed in through the high solid doors that seemed reluctant to admit anyone to the Club, long-serving member or not. He asked the porter to take his bags up to the room that had been booked for him and said that he would follow them up later. Dusk would soon be drawing in and he wanted to have a breath of fresh air while the sun was still out. With the beginning of spring it was possible that the little garden at the back of the Club might be open. He wandered through to the cocktail bar. Though he only rarely came to London these days, the staff still recognised him and were happy to open the French windows from the bar to the steep wrought iron fire escape that led down to the garden.

'What can I get for you, Mr Harvey,' asked the barman. 'Would you like to see the cocktail list?' The list of cocktails that the bar claimed to serve was impressive but a little fanciful. It was rare for any of the Club's elderly members to ask for a cocktail these days and Alec suspected that the list dated back to the thirties when his grandparents would come here overnight on one of their occasional periods of leave from Malawi.

'No thank you Gerry, just a G and T.' Gerry had been behind the bar as long as Alec could remember. He had always been a big man, but the red-faced bar tender was now so large that it was a wonder he could get in and out through the hatch. Perhaps he slept there standing up, thought Alec, wedged between the optics and never leaving his post. Gerry made the best gin and tonic in the world, intuitively without a measure, a large slug of Plymouth Gin with lots of ice, a slice of lime and a frozen glass, mixing it all with a theatrical flourish from his swizzle stick. Alec watched him take pleasure in his task. Gin and tonic had been his drink of choice since he could remember. The quinine in the tonic water had warded off malaria all his life, that at least was what Alec told himself, and the gin killed off all manner of bacteria. So the drink was strictly medicinal and as effective, he was convinced, as the mosquito coils that would burn every night through the house when as a child he visited his grandparents in Malawi, on their tobacco plantation outside Lilongwe on Lake Nyasa, the house boy creeping around with his matches every night to light them as dusk drew in. They were in tobacco, his grandparents; their descendents, his cousins, still keeping the plantations going in a now dwindling industry. Those had been the great days of the tobacco trade when everyone seemed to smoke and it had been a lucrative business. Now nobody seemed to smoke at all, at least not in public. This little cocktail bar at the Club used to be a fog of nicotine in the evening when everybody, even the women, lit up. Now only the yellowing stains on the ceiling gave testament to what seemed a bygone age.

As he thought of his grandparents, Alec descended to the garden and opened a new packet of Camel Lights. His grandparents, like his father, would use the Club for a night before catching their flight home after a visit to Kent. He would occasionally stay there himself as a child on his way to or from boarding school up in Shropshire. It had smelt musty even then. The creaks of the floorboards under the carpet were like old friends. In those days far from home, uncertain even where home was, the Club had been a reassuring haven in a topsy-turvy world. There were still one or two members of staff old enough to remember him as a child. They had seemed so grown up and competent to him when he was little, but they must have been much younger then than he was now. Alec still used the Club today as he had then. The beds creaked like the floors and the all-pervading quiet gave a sense of being cocooned out of time. His favourite room, high in the Club tucked away at the back in the eves of the building, gave him a glimpse of Buckingham Palace across Green Park. The chimes of Big Ben marked the passing quarters of the hour.

He enjoyed the cooling evening air in the garden as he sipped on his drink, smoked his cigarette and waited for someone to contact him as the Secretary had promised. The Club Secretary remained an elusive figure. He had to exist, after all Alec had spoken to him often enough on the telephone, indeed he had spoken to him only that morning, but Alec had never actually met him in all the years that he had been coming to Continental House or on any of his missions working for the Continental Club. Maybe the Secretary was not even based in that building but in some drab little Whitehall office or in a tower block in Croydon. Even in these days of 'transparency' where nothing seemed to be secret any longer, the Club and its Secretary remained stubbornly elusive.

In the little walled garden, secluded and hushed from the traffic of Piccadilly and the tourist chatter in Green Park just yards away, things were growing again. The bush that he had planted in the corner when his father had died was already in blossom. *Choisa trernata Sundance* it was called, a type of Mexican Orange blossom. He loved the tiny white flowers, the fact that it bloomed so early in the year before anything else was even in bud, a true sign that spring was about to arrive, and he loved the fact that it might unexpectedly break into flower again any time in the year, always when least expected. His father had bought him back a little Day of the Dead skeleton sculpture from Mexico when he was a child, a prized possession that still stood on his desk in his study. Planting this hardy evergreen all the way from Mexico had seemed a fitting way to remember him when he died. Alec loved the challenge of cultivating exotic plants in his corner of Kent: supplying the most luxurious and unlikely of blooms to his customers, the *strelitsias* of Southern Africa that Albert was keeping an eye on while he was away, with their unbelievable flowers and other such spectacularly vulgar wonders, but it was the exquisite white flowers on the Mexican Orange blossom that he loved best of all.

He was enjoying the last of the sun on his face when a voice called to him. 'Evening, Alec. Enjoying the sun? There'll be plenty more of that where you're going.'

He looked up and saw a familiar figure coming out of the bar.

'Hello André, what are you doing here?'

'Who else were you expecting?' came the reply through the big, bearded smile of someone who looked a most unlikely spymaster, fussy and breathless, uncomfortable in a ginger tweed suit as he tottered down the little black metal staircase to the garden.

'You were the last person I expected to see here. I thought you'd retired.'

'I have. But they brought me back to help out. Things are stretched at the moment. *Al Qaeda*, maverick nutters, Russia and a new cold war looming, Chechnya, still trouble in the Balkans, bloody Uncle Bob in Zim.... So I'm back as a freelancer. It's a reassuringly long contract for a man of my age. Anyway I was never one for retirement. Always have to be doing something or I drive myself mad.'

'I thought you hated London.'

'Too right I do, but needs must. I'm on my way back to South Africa and between planes. Thought I could use the time while I'm here to fill you in about where you're going.'

'And where am I going? Am I allowed to know?'

'Don't be like that. Surely the Secretary told you; you're off to Africa.'

'Africa's a bloody big place.'

'You're going to the bloody biggest bit of it. The Sudan. Africa within Africa the boys at your Foreign and Commonwealth Office call it. You don't need to go anywhere else for an African experience, everything the continent can offer is there.'

'Isn't there a war on?'

'There's always a war in the Sudan. Ever since you Brits left. Even before you got there come to that, which I suppose is why you went in the first place. Longest civil war in African history. It's been a north versus south thing for decades – blacks against Arabs, Muslims against Christians – but that's all fizzled out now for the most part and there's what they call the Comprehensive Peace Agreement in place. There's still trouble of course, warlords and bandits and now this business in Darfur.'

Alec had heard about that on the radio. 'Isn't that pretty bad?' he asked.

'You don't know the half of it. Religion, oil, the Chinese, the French, American spies pretending to be missionaries, missionaries pretending to be spies, countries all around being drawn into it.'

'You don't expect me to sort it out, do you?'

'Of course not. It's a right bloody mess, but it's a sideshow. It'll go on for ever. No, we have got a particular little problem we'd like you to deal with.'

André's drink arrived, a low alcohol beer brought on a silver tray by a young waiter from one of the East European states that André had devoted his life to spying on. They sat together in silence. No doubt the bar staff had all been vetted and signed the Official Secrets Act, but it was always best to be cautious. The waiter disappeared inside and André began.

'Our sources have told us that something is going on, a plot of some sort out of the Sudan. How do we know? Chatter, just chatter my boy. You know, little bits and pieces we pick up, overheard conversations, mobile phone intercepts, gossip frankly, some of it. We only have the barest details but we do know that it's got to be stopped. Your job is to get out to Khartoum, infiltrate and terminate; simple as that, in and out. You've got a couple of days at most, that's why you're booked onto tomorrow night's flight. There are only two a week and by the time the next one goes it will all be too late.'

'Foil a plot André. What sort of a plot?'

'Sorry Alec, we just don't know. You'll meet our man on the ground when you get there and he'll be able to give you what we do know. What we can say is that it is almost certainly something to do with oil. Of that much we are pretty sure. It's a toxic mix of oil and religion out there and with the war supposedly over and the place being divvied up through the peace process, everyone wants to get their hands on the reserves. The Americans had pretty much left the place alone, they got their fingers badly burnt in Somalia and had their embassy blown up in Kenya, so it's not been their favourite part of the world. They've still got a trade embargo so that's left it open to the Chinese who are there in a big way. The Yanks are just beginning to realise they might have been beaten to it.'

'And the British?' Alec asked.

'BP are there of course. They always kept an interest even through the worst of the fighting. That's why British Airways have kept flying empty planes to Khartoum every week.' André was relaxing now. The modest amount of alcohol in his beer was having an effect. 'There's something else that has got the Americans interested. The religious right have come to see the place as a new frontier. Between the Christians in the south and the Muslims in the north. Between Arabs and Africans. There's a simple truth in that and you know how much the Americans like their politics simple. You can guess which side they are on. Despite the war it's been a stable country in some ways and looks like becoming more stable still with the possibility of a lasting peace.'

'Despite what's happening in Darfur?' asked Alec.

'Yes, it's terrible of course but no worse than what has been going on in the rest of the country for the last thirty years. It's only the looming peace elsewhere and the freeing up of the oil reserves that has made the West take notice. But some in America aren't happy at the Arabs continuing to have the upper hand and subjugating their Christian brothers in the south. There's still missionary work to be done in Africa and the Americans of the mid-West are a far more determined lot than Livingstone ever was.'

'And the oil?'

'Some of the best reserves in the world and the West have neglected them. Too busy sucking up to the Saudis and making a mess of things on the other side of the Gulf in the Middle East. The country has been left wide open for the Chinese. They've been quietly there for years. Building dams and refineries. There's a fortune to be made from the oil and it's becoming ever more important with supplies threatened elsewhere. Have you seen the barrel price today? The futures prices would make your hair fall out. There are plenty of people who would like to see things upset, militant Islamists mostly who don't see the present government as being radical enough and really don't want a peace with the south that will lead to any sort of power sharing. They want *Sharia* law for all and the Horn of Africa could easily go their way. It's happening in Somalia, could easily happen in Ethiopia, and Sudan is already half-way there.'

Alec lit another cigarette as André went on.

'Oil and Islam, it's a toxic brew and somewhere a shadowy character is stirring it. That's who you've got to find. We know almost nothing about him, perhaps not even *that* much if I'm honest. He's some sort of a mastermind and there is lots of chatter about him but no hard facts. We thought he was a Saudi dissident like old Osama Bin Laden or maybe a new *Mahdi*.'

'A *Mahdi*, André?'

'Yes. Come on you're the Arabist. It means 'the rightly guided one' chosen to turn the whole world Muslim. He's not alone this guy; that we do know. There are others with him, collected from all over the place. He's a magnet. We hear about him popping up all over Africa but hardly anyone has seen him. What we do know, and this is the important bit, is that he is going to use the *Moulid* as a cover for this plot of his.'

Alec stopped him.

'The what it?' he asked.

'The *Moul-lid*,' he articulated the d, 'like the top of a bowl of mussels. A *Moulid* is a birthday and this is a special one, the *Moulid El-Bay*, The Prophet's birthday. It's a big bash in Khartoum, people come from all over. Every type of Muslim you could imagine.'

Alec confessed that he'd never heard of it.

'Why would you have done? Not every country celebrates

it. It's even forbidden in Saudi. But in Sudan it's the biggest festival of the year – Christmas, Thanksgiving, you name it, all rolled into one.'

'When is it?' Alec asked, realising as he did so that he probably knew the answer.

'This week. It's a three day affair. Starts on Wednesday. If this chap succeeds in whatever he has planned for Sudan who knows what it will lead to. Fancy another drink?'

It all seemed a bit far fetched to Alec, sitting here in an English garden rattling the fragments of ice melting in the bottom of what remained of his gin and tonic. 'I'll get them. Same again?' He was glad of an excuse to go up to the bar and let his head clear. There was a lot to think about.

'Are we sure of his plan?' he asked when he returned with the drinks. 'To destabilise the whole region and convert the world to Islam?' Alec immediately regretted using the plural; by saying 'we' he had included himself and realised that it meant that he had committed himself to being a part of whatever André was planning. After a couple of years of a quiet life in the country he was again about to play in Kipling's 'Great Game'. He wondered what he was letting himself in for.

'We're not sure of anything. That's why we're sending you.'

'What were you saying about the *Mahdi*?'

'He could be the new prophet, the reincarnation of the guy who gave the Brits all those problems a century ago. You remember.'

'I wasn't there.'

'Yes, but you know what I mean. There was a *Mahdi* who caused no end of trouble for the British in Khartoum a hundred years ago. Queen Victoria had to send General Gordon out to stop him and it led to a right bloody mess.'

Alec had a vague idea, though history, like French and German, was never a strong point at school. But he had a memory of a blacked-up Laurence Olivier as a rather camp Arab opposite Charlton Heston's equally unlikely English general in a movie about the British defeat in Sudan.

'It's not a new thing. Tradition has it that a *Mahdi* will appear before the end of time and convert the whole world to the way of Islam. Plenty of people claiming to be the *Mahdi* have popped up since the time of The Prophet. The guy in Khartoum wasn't the first and he's certainly not been the last. There was one in Saudi in the seventies and there have been a few in Iraq since the war. Old Ahmadinezhad prays publicly for one to turn up in Iran. So if it is someone claiming to be the *Mahdi*, maybe even believing he is the *Mahdi*, he could cause real trouble.'

'Is that what I tell them at the airport in Khartoum? "I'm here to stop the *Mahdi*." I can't see it going down too well.'

'Of course not. We've booked you to give a talk for the British Council.'

'On what?' Alec asked.

'Gardening, of course. Giving a talk on horticulture. You can tell them about your work in the nurseries and give them a bit of advice on what to grow in their little gardens. It's all a bit last minute but I'm sure you'll get a decent crowd at the Council offices. It's a perfect cover. You're very popular you know, answering your gardeners' questions on the BBC. You've got quite a following. They love gardening out there. I guess it's because there's so little they can grow for themselves in all that dust. The expat community will adore you; they'll have heard of you on 'Gardeners' Question Time'. That and 'The Archers' are the most popular programmes out there. The Arabs listen on their short band radios and the Brits listen on their computers. The Sudanese will probably love it even more than the Brits.'

'What about the flight? Won't I have to spend a night in Nairobi or somewhere?'

'There's a BA flight out tomorrow. They've only just started flying the route again after the last bit of trouble but business is picking up for them and the Foreign Office is slipping them something to keep the route open so we've had no problem getting you a seat.'

'And what about a visa?' He knew how difficult they could be to obtain in that part of the world.

'Don't worry, we applied weeks ago through the Ambassador just in case this all came to a head. Leave your passport with Judy at the PR office at the Club tonight and she'll sort it out first thing, straight after morning prayers at the Embassy while you're at the Foreign Office. There's a new junior minister there who will bring you up to date with the politics and give you the official line. She's not exactly up to speed herself so don't expect too much. Number Ten holds all the cards these days so she probably knows less than I do, but it's protocol to see her. I'd hoped to get you a meeting at the Cabinet Office but no can do. They're too busy with rebellious backbenchers to have time for anything happening overseas.'

It was beginning to get chilly and so, business done, they clambered up the steps to the bar and ordered themselves another drink. Alec asked about André's seemingly endless extended family with his countless grandchildren and Isobel, his long-suffering wife, who quietly held the fort back home while her husband jaunted around the globe fixing international crises that never made it onto a front page. Their drinks finished, they gave a cheery goodbye to Gerry who was polishing glasses behind the bar and walked out into the chill evening air. André made his way to Green Park tube station to catch the last flight to Jo'burg and Alec strolled in the other direction, along Jermyn Street, past the windows full of shirts and cigars and shaving cream, towards Regent Street.

He crossed Piccadilly Circus and merged into the crowds thronging the theatres of Shaftesbury Avenue. As darkness began to set in behind the blaze of neon it started to rain, a light warm drizzle cleaning the air. The rain became more persistent as he turned left into Soho and he wished he'd thought to bring an umbrella. Pulling his collar up he wandered through the narrow streets trying to remember which of the many corners the little Moroccan restaurant he had remembered was on. For a while Soho had been a virtual second home to him when he was living in London and freelancing for the BBC World Service. In the World Service, funded as it was directly by the British Government, a freelancer was another word for someone who worked as much for the government as they did for the BBC. Alec had just been a journalist for hire, plucked from his fellow students at a graduate recruitment fair. While his friends had been wandering around fantasising about possible lives for themselves once they left university and avoiding the stalls promoting the less glamorous possibilities, Alec had been discretely approached and taken aside for a drink. A family friend must have suggested him, at least that was what he had always assumed, probably old Uncle Leo. He never had to fill in an application form, just found himself being called from Bush House to come in and help out in the Arabic service or on a magazine programme using his knowledge of the language and of life in Cairo. First it had just been the odd piece here and there, then it led to trips overseas, and later to being asked by someone at the British Council to deliver a message or a package like a human diplomatic bag. As the months went by he came to realise that he never quite knew who he was working for. Paid by the BBC World Service, which was of course itself paid by the Foreign and Commonwealth Office, and doing the odd errand for the FCO or the British Council. As a freelancer though, he was technically only ever working for himself and never in the service of any one organisation. He guessed that was how all freelancers worked – for themselves, or for one government or another or perhaps for more than one. It had all been a complex tangle of politics that he only began to understand when André came to take him under his wing, introduced him to the Continental Club and his real work began. As he walked in the rain it occurred to Alec that he never really knew which of the many things he did was his real work. It dawned on him that even the guest spots on 'Gardeners' Question Time' might be another front set up years ago just in case it was ever needed in a situation like this.

He was sure the restaurant had been on a corner, but which one? There were so many new restaurants and bars since he had last been in Soho. Greek Street, Dean Street, Frith Street. He tried to recall which was which as they came off Old Compton Street. He was just about to give up when he saw it, the little entrance hidden away with a heavy carved wooden door that could have been out of a story from the Arabian Nights. He might not have noticed it at all but for the three raucous and very drunk young women sitting outside under a gas heater smoking on a *shisha* pipe. He guessed that you were not allowed to smoke even those indoors any more. Alec smiled at the girls as he pulled at the door and disappeared inside, glad to get out of the wet.

As the door closed behind him it was suddenly very dark and it took his eyes a while to get accustomed to the gloom. After a moment or two it all came back to him, though it must have been three or four years since he was last there. In front of him a vertiginous and familiar staircase led down to a large cellar elaborately decorated with cushions, *shisha* pipes, and densely-patterned but very well-worn carpets. A couple of Middle Eastern businessmen were chatting quietly in a far corner and some students were spread out along a low table enjoying a *meze* of foods in ornate bowls. Alec had expected the place to be buzzing with Arabs but maybe the fact of its being a Saturday and evening prayers not long over accounted for the quietness. He would be lucky to practice much Arabic tonight. Or so he thought as he dropped down on an especially large cushion and ordered a cocktail from the waiter. In the old days he would have sipped a mint tea and ordered a pipe like the girls outside, and filled the air around him with its fruity smoke, but tonight, unable to smoke, he succumbed instead to an elaborate cocktail. Alec was wrong about the Arabic. A large figure loomed from the side of the bar, improbably dressed in a white suit and ruby-red fez, unlikely garb even for Soho on a Saturday night, and stood over him.

'*Masaa el kheer*, Mr Alec,' a voice whispered from the shadowy figure. 'We haven't seen you for a long, long while. I trust all is well – *Kaifa haloka*?'

'*Ana bekhair, shokran!* I'm very well indeed. So you're still running this place you old rogue?'

The shadowy figure gently lowered his vast frame onto a stool next to him. Now Alec could make out his features, coloured from the thick glass in the many lamps that hung from the low ceiling and flickering in the light from the guttering candles on the table.

'*Maharban* my English friend!' The bar's owner welcomed him back as if he had never been away.

'So Aazad, how's tricks? You're quiet tonight.'

'It is yet but early. Once the theatres close the place you see will be packed. Drunken young women lying on my every cushion. I have no reason to complain. And you, Mr Alec, what has taken you from us and what is it that brings you back?'

Alec was so pleased to see the fat old Moroccan that he almost told him the truth. But instead they made small talk and Alec polished his rusty Arabic. They chatted about life in the countryside growing seeds and life in London running a bar, a bar that had looked as if it had seen better days from the moment it opened, at a time when Soho was a place of milk bars and teddy boys and the Maltese still ran the sex industry. The two of them had known each other for years, since Alec first descended that staircase as a wide-eyed student. Then it had been a strange and wonderful place to go, a hidden haunt for all manner of exiles. London was a different place now and Aazad's 'Scheherazade Bar' had become a place not for Arabs, they had moved to the Edgware Road, but for tourists who stumbled upon it in awed amazement after watching a big musical in the theatre across the street.

Time floated by and the bar began to fill. Aazad went off to sort out some business in the kitchens telling Alec as he went that he had a surprise in store. A moment or two later blaring music from a CD player behind the bar announced the surprise and the door in the corner under the stairs swung open as a belly dancer entered the room, the kitchen creating a shimmering tableau with a background of brightness and white tiles and steam behind her. For a moment Alec's eyes were dazzled and then the door swung closed behind her and the light from a thousand pieces of coloured glass played on the dancer's body. The businessmen in the corner continued their intense conversation as if nothing had happened while the rest of the punters clapped with pleasure. Alec was enchanted even though he had seen many belly dancers before – his uncle had introduced him to that world on his first visit to Cairo where Leo's taste for big bellies had been easily and often satisfied. Alec's taste was for something slimmer than his uncle had required and he found the girl from the kitchen delightful. She danced with great skill but had little of the Middle East about her looks. Alec doubted that she had ever been further east than Southend and was probably dancing to pay her way through college. Her pale, very English skin had not seen the sun all winter and there was certainly no natural light to reach it in the basement bar. As she moved across the floor the girl appeared almost phosphorescent, like some strange creature of the deep on the Discovery Channel. English she might be but she knew all the moves and her skinny frame, so unlike the rolling stomach of the Egyptian dancers his uncle favoured, was strangely attractive. Alec watched in wonder at her pale, translucent flesh as he sipped on his drink.

She did a circuit of the bar, shimmering her tassels at him as she went by and her belly jewel dislodged itself and plopped into his glass. Embarrassed, she withdrew back into the kitchen just as Aazad was coming out. Alec asked him where he had found her. 'She was working at the strip club up the road – well you know how it is,' he sighed and shrugged his shoulders, 'I'm not getting any younger and the spirit might be willing but the flesh is weak. So, a little window shopping in the afternoon when the bar is quiet and I've nothing else to do is all I can hope for. She seemed wasted there on a tiny stage with a few ancient footlights and a tatty velvet curtain. So I asked Mr B if he would let her come and work for me.' Aazad was a truly Falstaffian figure, a Moroccan quoting Shakespeare in his 'Scheherazade Bar' under the streets of London.

The belly dancer returned in a while complete with a new jewel glued into her navel for another dance. Later, after she had finished her work, Aazad introduced her. 'Gemma, you must meet my old friend Mr Alec. He is a connoisseur of the dance.'

'Really? Well I hope you like what you saw.'

In her jeans and tee shirt, her hair tied tightly back, she was a different woman, a girl even.

'It was a delight,' he answered truthfully. 'Where did you learn?'

Gemma turned out to be a student at a dance school in Islington and was living nearby in Covent Garden. Azad left them alone and went to cash up the till. They chatted over a couple of beers; a conversation that did nothing to improve his Arabic but would have been useful if he had been going undercover in Essex. The night was coming to an end and as Aazad began to blow out the candles, Alec offered to walk Gemma home. The old Moroccan pulled himself up the stairs to see them off into the night. '*Tosbeho,* Mr Alec,' he wheezed, '*Araki fima ba'd* my dear.'

'*Ma'a salama,* Aazad,' Alec clasped the old man to his chest and kissed him on both cheeks.

They made love on the futon on the floor of her room. Her feet and ankles were still covered with the henna tattoos she had applied for her act, intricate patterns of brown dots like mazes of freckles. As she gasped beneath him he caught site of them out of the corners of his eyes. He noticed another tattoo on her thigh, permanent in that peculiar greenish blue dye. Her belly button was pierced, red and sore where her dancing chain had been, a scar hidden by the jewel that had landed in his drink. As his mouth moved down between her thighs he realised that it was not only her belly button that was pierced. The tattoos and jewellery emphasised her nakedness and added to the strange exoticism of this encounter in her student digs, her flatmates no doubt listening – or trying not to listen – in the kitchen next door. They came together and fell apart lying next to each other and disappearing for a while into their own worlds. 'What are you thinking about,' she wanted to know. He told her about Cairo and his Uncle Leo, half a world away, where he had first seen women with tattooed feet dancing in the sand. She was entranced by his tales. It had been one of the happiest times of his life and he joyed in remembering it with her, everything from watching the belly dancers with Uncle Leo to the terrifying thrill of camel racing in the desert.

It was the early hours by the time he made it back to the Club. His bags were waiting in his room but he was too tired to unpack. He pulled off his clothes, slid between the crisp sheets and was asleep in seconds.

* * *

The steward had to knock hard on the door next morning to wake him for his breakfast. Alec treated himself to a full English breakfast in bed, with carrot juice on the side, a meal that he would not be able to get again until he returned from his trip, and perused the papers in the hope of finding a snippet of news relevant to what was happening in Africa. Finding nothing he showered, dressed and set off for his meeting with the Minister at the Foreign and Commonwealth Office.

The sun was out and London was slowly coming to life, a few tourists here and there peering at their maps. He strolled slowly through the park as he had time to spare before his meeting. The guard was changing on Horse Guards Parade. The fountains dazzled in the light and the grass was as green as could be. A pelican eyed him quizzically. Alec peered at the sign telling him that the birds had originally been brought to St James's Park as a gift from the Russian Ambassador in the seventeenth century. Alec wondered whether there really had been Pelicans in seventeenth century Russia and whether these birds were their descendents or new ones from Africa.

Alec had never been to the Foreign Office before and it took him a while to find the right building amid the Victorian edifices around Whitehall that all looked anonymously the same. He walked around the block and at first went into the Treasury. The security guard there did not even know what building he was working in, let alone which building might be the Foreign and Commonwealth Office. 'I just work for the agency mate,' he told Alec, loyal to the firm employing him rather than Her Majesty's Government.

He was still early when he eventually found where he was going and had time to wander around the magnificent interior while he waited for his appointment. Gilbert Scott's building was a fabulous thing – unchanged and, if anything, more glamorous now than it had been when it was opened with a reception for the Sultan of Turkey in the Great Courtyard in

1867. His great grandfather had been there that day and now here was Alec, three generations later, staring around in wonder at the decoration all about him. His ancestor would have found it even more splendid now, lit by electric light. No expense had been spared in building the Foreign Office and no expense had been spared in refurbishing it for its twenty-first century occupants even though the Empire it was built to administer had disappeared long ago. There had been the great triumvirate of the Foreign Office, the India Office and the Colonial Office in the Empire's heyday. Now the Foreign and Commonwealth Office that was left behind still saw the world as a colony that needed regular paternalist interference from London.

All the tea and carrot juice he had drunk at breakfast was working its way through him and he made for the toilets, expecting some tiled Victorian grandeur. He was disappointed; the old toilets had been stripped out and replaced with something modern and anaemic. There was a huge stall built for wheelchair access, something that was definitely not a part of Gilbert Scott's original design, though how a disabled person would get up here to the top of the Great Staircase was a mystery. A female security guard passed him as he came out of the toilet, another modern incongruity, and like the black African and Sikh staff at the cloakroom and at the door, she wore the uniform of a private security firm. Another woman, this time in a military uniform, had a sub-machine gun slung over her shoulder. Some of the extras and the toilets might have changed but their setting was as it had always been.

He kicked his heels in the Locarno Room as he waited for the baroness to see him. The whole room was brightly lit by chandeliers, the gold leaf on the walls glistening and the letters VR springing out in huge relief on the wall above him. The clocked ticked slowly in the mantle, taking no account of what he assumed to be the urgency of his mission. The minister seemed in no hurry either, though her presence in the office on a Sunday morning when everyone else had long retired for the weekend must mean something. The life peers always seemed to get the jobs in government no-one else wanted. Eventually a door opened and a figure came in to greet him. To his shame it took him a moment to realise that this was the minister. He had expected a woman after what André had told him, but he had not expected someone so attractive or so black. He wondered what part of the old empire she came from.

'I'm told you are our man,' she said as they sat in plump chairs under a portrait of some long forgotten diplomat. 'Glad you can do this for us.'

'I'm still a little hazy as to what it is I'm being asked to do.'

'Sort things out. Find this fellow and stop him doing whatever it is he is planning to do.'

She made it seem so simple.

'Is it really that straightforward? It's a big country you know.'

'I do know my geography, and a little history, Alec,' she replied with a familiarity that grated on him. Perhaps she thought he was patronising her. 'That part of the world is my speciality. That's why they gave me the post here. I lectured in colonial history before becoming involved in politics, you know.'

He did not know. 'My apologies,' he said trying to get the conversation back on track, 'I'm just finding this whole mission a little vague.'

'That's the challenge. My officials tell me you're the man for the job, just as they advised Lord Salisbury all those years ago. I hope their advice this time is better.'

He looked blank. 'I'm sorry?'

' "If you want some out-of-the-way piece of work to be done in an unknown and barbarous country, Gordon would be your man." That's what they told Salisbury.'

'I'm no General Gordon, minister.'

'I do hope not Alec, we're not the colonial power any more. Tread carefully out there, we don't want an incident.'

She was beginning to really irritate him now and if he had not said to André that he would do the job he might have got up and walked out there and then.

'I'll do my best, Minister, and tread as carefully as I can.'

'Good, that's what we want. Sort out whatever it is that is planned for this week and get back to London before anyone has noticed you've been away. Just a couple of things: don't get the Embassy involved, it's all far too delicate. The PM doesn't know anything about this and we want to keep it that way. That's why we've sub-contracted and got the Club involved.'

'Is there any back up or am I on my own?'

'Not much I'm afraid Alec. We haven't even got a World Service stringer out there any more. But the British Council man will do what he can and I'm sure the Club will have someone on hand.'

He stood to go and shook her hand.

'One last thing,' she called back to him as he was opening the door. He gritted his teeth.

'Could I ask you to sign this?'

Surely you they did not expect him to sign the Official Secrets Act after all these years, he thought as he turned back to her. She looked slightly embarrassed as she slid a copy of a gardening book across her vast desk.

'My mother listens to you on the radio all the time. She'll be so impressed that I've met you.'

CHAPTER TWO

Airborne

Kati Johnson had done the London-Khartoum flight many times now. It was still her favourite despite all the dangers of flying in and out of war-torn Sudan. Working on an airplane had always seemed such a romantic thing to her and even now with years of experience behind her the romance remained. As a schoolgirl it had been her only thought: so many places to go, people to see and always somewhere to escape to from the boredom of life in England. Kati had worked hard at school and had a gift for languages that she pursued rigorously. Not just French, which was compulsory, and German, which was a common second option, but she had done a little Spanish too; then, when an Arabic speaking chemistry teacher arrived at the school, she took lessons from him. She quickly fell in love with the language and with the culture and mystery of which it was a part and the romance that in her imagination went with it.

She had watched 'Lawrence of Arabia' as a sixth former and fallen head over heels in love with Omar Sharif, the first big crush in her life and one that had defined her relationships ever since. It was the difference that excited her, the complete otherness of Arabia. She knew, even when she was sixteen and staring up at Peter O'Toole and Sharif on the cinema screen, that the Arab world would somehow become a part of her life, even if, as a teenager at a girls' boarding school in Sussex, she did not yet know quite how. She might not have had T. E. Lawrence's opportunities in a long forgotten war or O'Toole's chances to go on location with film crews, but for a girl there was always British Airways. She never went very far as a schoolgirl, rarely travelled. It was her father who did that on one overseas posting after another, a distant figure who would return home once in a while with a gift, a memento of where he had been. She collected them carefully, as the most precious of possessions, and knew for certain that one day she too would go to those far away places from which he returned with such wonderful gifts. She knew it as she became the first British schoolgirl to take Arabic A-level, knew it through university, and she knew it when she began her training with BA in a far from romantic office block outside of Heathrow.

The other girls were there for all sorts of reasons: for the glamour of it, for the uniform, for the romance, or for the sex that inevitably came with the overnight lay-offs on the long haul flights. The rumours of the endless party-going in Hong Kong were especially enticing for some of her colleagues. But Kati was different. She never much enjoyed the partying, or even the flights themselves come to that. It was not the travel that she loved but the being somewhere else at the end of it. She took all the less popular routes and while others wanted the plum flights to Las Vegas, L.A., New York, Cape Town or Sydney, she would happily trade when those routes came her way for the other dusty, sweaty locations that no-one else wanted like Lagos, Nairobi, Kampala or best of all the Middle East or somewhere in Arab Africa. These were the flights everybody else hated working because for the rest of the crews they had no glamour at all and were the last places on earth that flight crews wanted to have to spend a night. Her willingness to trade shifts made her popular, but also set her apart from the others who manned the cabins. And all this because of that chemistry teacher from Syria, a political refugee who had offered to teach Arabic in a girls' boarding school in the south of England as a way of keeping in touch with his own language.

It was not just the sounds of Arabic that she liked. She loved the look of the script, the beauty of the writing and the perversity of everything being back to front. Her classmates at school had been mystified by her but then she had gone on to London to read Arabic at the School of Oriental and African Studies and immersed herself in the Arab world. Even the acronym by which the college was known, SOAS, sounded foreign and mysterious and she met the most astonishing collection of people there, making friends around the world. When she finished with a very good degree the obvious routes for her had been the Foreign Office or the academic world, but Kati had always been active and loved to travel and had always had this fantasy of being on a crew for British Airways. So she signed up with the airline, and her managers had thought themselves lucky to have someone with her language skills prepared to work in the cabins. Her looks were no doubt a bonus too: long blonde hair and even longer legs were always welcome on board long haul flights. Though it was the destinations not the flying she loved, she was prepared to spend hours pushing a trolley three thousand feet in the air just to reach those places. While her friends from SOAS were going off to work for oil companies and banks where their knowledge of Arabic and the Arab world would quickly earn them fabulous salaries, she was in that bleak training centre in Hounslow learning how to pour cups of coffee during turbulence and how to escape a smoke filled cabin in the middle of the Atlantic.

Kati had been sorry when the twice-weekly flights to Sudan had been suspended. They had become a regular part of her life and a way of keeping in touch with a country she had got to know for one long and magical summer between university and beginning work with the airline. She had worked for an American charity, Trans World Aid, in the refugee camps around Khartoum. It had been serendipity that took her there. She had applied to all sorts of places and organisations, but it was the American Christians who needed her, and though she professed no faith herself (her parents had been social members of the Anglican Church and she had only ever gone to church for weddings and funerals) she did believe in seizing opportunities and a job in the Sudan was an opportunity to seize. No longer would her experience of the Arab world be confined to the Middle East; Trans World Aid would take her deep into the heart of Africa.

It had not immediately been an easy country to fall in love with, and it had not been the easiest place to be a tall, blonde, white woman. Soon however she came to relish being caught between the black African, Christian, chaotic world of the refugee camps and the very different world of Islamist order of the city proper. Not that any of her colleagues on the flight tonight would know anything of either world. If she had stuck to the routine offered by the airline she too would not know that the country she had experienced as a student existed at all. But Kati had always found a way to escape from the dreary predictability of the hotels the crews were assigned on long stopovers and was able to do that even more so in Khartoum where the length of the stopovers gave her plenty of time to get out and explore, even if sometimes it had to be with a male driver and discretely dressed.

On this flight she was able to enjoy the relative luxury of working the first class cabin, although it did mean having to put up with the unwanted attentions of Geoffrey, the captain. They had first met, and a brief romance had blossomed, on the Hong Kong route. There was something crazy and hedonistic about those stopovers in Hong Kong in the months before handover. With so much sex, booze and cocaine and so little sleep it was a wonder any of the crew ever did the return leg. Indeed there were some who never did make it back, at least not working the flights. One young cabin attendant returned a different sex to the one he had flown out as which had caused no end of complications with his passport at the British Consulate. Hong Kong was long ago and Kati could enjoy Geoff's company once in a while on a flight but wished he did not still harbour hopes of their getting back together. Life had moved on and Geoffrey was not the man for her; indeed she winced now when she admitted to herself that she had ever gone out with him.

It was quiet in the first class cabin tonight, as it was most nights on this route. Just a couple of UN officials with their pale blue passports, a Sudanese businessman and a middle-aged American woman clutching what seemed to be a bible tightly in her lap throughout the flight. Kati guessed she must be a nervous flyer and went to ask if she needed anything.

'Only the love of our Lord Jesus Christ,' was the response. 'Are you a believer my dear?'

Kati could not think of an easy reply and found herself saying, 'Not really.'

'There is no easy way to say this, my dear,' the woman replied, 'but I am afraid that if you do not believe in our Lord Jesus Christ you will be condemned to burn forever in the fires of damnation.'

Kati left the woman a blanket and did not bother her again.

She did a last round of drinks before the lights went out and wandered back into economy to check that everything was alright with the rest of the cabin crew. It was no busier back there, just a Sudanese family of women and children all in Islamic dress but no men with them (perhaps that was the husband up in first class), a few young Chinese in smart new suits, African men travelling alone, and a rather attractive European man in crumpled linen suit and seriously in need of a shave. She noticed that he had a slightly swarthy look, an open air type, and was well tanned. He caught her eye and they smiled at each other as she turned on her heel and went back to the galley.

She pulled down a seat, sat down and closed her eyes. This would be the only opportunity to doze on the flight. By the time the passengers had been fed and watered there were only a few hours before breakfast had to be served. No-one flew to Khartoum for pleasure so it was very businesslike at both ends of the plane. Everyone on the flight, cabin crew as well as passengers, was glad to get some rest. She realised that she must have fallen asleep when she felt one of her colleagues shaking her by the shoulder and telling her that it was time to serve breakfast. She stretched and poured herself a large orange juice and a coffee before going to wake and serve her passengers. Everyone was dozing except for the family and the first class businessman who were quietly saying prayers as dawn broke through the left-hand cabin windows. She knew from experience that there was dispensation on long flights, indeed on any travel, about obligations to observe the call to prayer. With time differences and the difficulty of facing Mecca to pray, there had to be a degree of pragmatism in the religious observance of the modern Muslim.

It only took a while to finish the stocktaking as the flight came to an end. Ten hours with so few passengers, hardly anyone drinking alcohol and no-one buying duty free, meant there was very little paperwork to be done. The route could scarcely pay its way, she thought. Maybe the government discretely financed it or maybe the airline saw it as an investment for the future when the US lifted their trade embargo and British Petroleum got heavily involved again. It was the BP trade that was keeping Virgin's flights to Nigeria in healthy profit she had heard.

'Cabin crew, prepare for landing.' Geoff's voice again. As she heard it she remembered when she had first seen him, how much she wanted to be with him that day flying to Hong Kong and how little she wanted to be with him today years later flying into Khartoum. It took a while for the ground crew to wheel the steps up to the plane and Kati peered through the window of the door to catch a glimpse of Africa as she waited. Then, when the ground crew were ready, she swung the handle to the door and pushed it open, a huge gust of warm air hitting her in the face. 'Goodbye, goodbye, goodbye,' she repeated with a fixed smile as the plane emptied. The UN officials were off first and she saw them being whisked away in a gleaming new white Range Rover the moment their feet touched the tarmac. The American woman, still clutching her bible, was next and then the Sudanese man who was having trouble reaching down an aluminium flight case from the locker above his seat. He got quite angry with her when she tried to help. She stayed as the rest of the passengers left from the back of the plane and caught the eye of the man she had noticed last night. She watched him light up a cigarette as soon as he stepped onto the tarmac.

The large extended Sudanese family were the last to leave, trailing after their man from first class. He was probably a high ranking government official, maybe even a junior minister, thought Kati; no other Sudanese would either be allowed to travel or be able to afford to, certainly not in first class even if the rest of his family were in economy. As soon as they left, Kati did the last bit of paper work and with the others was off the plane as well.

Even as air crew they had to deal with some of the formalities that every African airport, north or south of the Sahara, seemed to love: little bits of paper to be stuck into passports and colourful rubber stamps. There were no bribes though, at least not that she was aware of. Perhaps the airline dealt with those for them, or maybe the British Airways representative in Khartoum bought everybody off as part of his job.

For the rest of the crew, Khartoum was usually just a one night stopover in the Meridien Hotel with a bottle of duty free if one could get it past the officials who blighted the lives of everyone, even the air crews, as they came into the country. Kati had been flying the route whenever she could since it was reinstated after the last bout of troubles ebbed, always avoiding the Meridien and booking privately into the Parthenon to which she could sneak away while the others were sleeping off the effects of the night flight. It was the hotel she had stayed in when she first came to the city on that trip after university and it had come to be a second home for her. She did not count her fellow crew members as intimate friends but rather remained just close enough to lubricate a working relationship. The airline had the rooms booked at the international hotel, just as they had rooms booked at every destination, and were not about to pay for Kati to stay somewhere else. That sort of freedom was not even an option officially. Unofficially, however, all sorts of things happened and crew members were known to stay everywhere from transvestite brothels in Bangkok to boutique hotels in New York and crack houses in Mexico City. Kati might not have been to those extremes but she had stayed at the Parthenon many times when she was younger and always preferred to stay there now when she was working, slipping away once she was registered at the grander, bland international hotel by the Nile.

They did not have to wait for their ride into town. Amidst the battered, bright yellow Toyota Corollas and the six-seater minivans that were hustling for trade at the airport was their usual hotel driver waiting to meet them with a smart white taxi ready to take them straight to the hotel through the mid-morning heat. The traffic was bumper-to-bumper as everyone tried to get their business done before either the call to prayer or the midday heat that would soon be so insufferable that it would bring everything to a standstill. Being a hotel taxi, it was much grander than everything else that was on the dusty streets, certainly the tiny three-wheeled taxis, the *bajajis*, that hurtled all around them as they got nearer to the centre of town. Their taxi must just have been cleaned for it gleamed in comparison to the vehicles surrounding them. The dust, the dust. She had forgotten how it got everywhere, coating all the vehicles, getting through every gap and clogging up the air conditioning so that cars were covered with dust inside and out.

The route from the airport took them straight into town, glancing by the Nile just before they reached the hotel. She had had no chance to see the river from the plane, but suddenly there it was stretching lazily in front of her, the most famous river in the world. The hotel was just back from its banks, close to where the two great tributaries, the Blue and White Niles, converged.

She remembered her first sight of Nile when she arrived for her volunteer work with Trans World Aid. She had heard so much about it even at school. Heard how Khartoum was a unique melting pot, a place where Arabia meets Africa, where east meets west, and where the Blue Nile and the White Nile meet and merge in what Arab poets call 'the longest kiss in history' to create the huge expanse of moving water that dominates this city in the desert. Even from where she was standing as she got out of the car she could see the clearly different colours of the Blue and White Nile. Each, she had come to learn, had their different characters and origins and her fascination with the river and its stories had never dulled.

Once inside the doors of the hotel she could have been in any city at the end of any flight. She guessed there was something comforting about these hotels for those westerners who were always travelling but never wanted to leave home. A little huddle of NGO workers was in one corner chatting over coffee but otherwise the place was deserted. After they had done the formalities of the front desk, she said goodbye to the others, making a half-hearted promise to meet them later, and once they were out of sight went outside to the taxi which was still in front of the hotel, its driver wiping the dust that was already coating its windows, and asked to be taken straight to her other hotel.

Andreas, the manager, was a good friend of all the airlines; many of their bookings came through the little agency he ran from his cramped office. Everyone coming to Khartoum, journalists, aid workers, mercenaries, adventurers, passed through his hotel. There seemed to be nothing that Andreas could not arrange. Even when the front of the hotel was blown in by a bomb in 1987, life had gone on as if nothing had happened. In fact if anything, life had been busier. The journalists in the hotel were finally able to write about something that they had witnessed first hand, rather than pass on the second-hand gossip that they usually recycled. For Kati it was a safe and familiar place to stay.

The air conditioning rattled nosily in the corner of her room. It had been put on its highest setting ready for her arrival and the room was positively chilly. She switched it off and felt the heat creep into the room. The silence around her was emphasized by the soft, dulled sounds outside the shuttered windows. Sounds of traffic and of people distorted in the shimmering heat as it rose and rippled from the dry dust and hot tarmac.

She showered and washed the smells of the flight from her body. So hot was it in the hotel that even the cold water was warm. She stepped back into the bedroom, glimpsing her body in the cracked mirror, noticing the slight sag in her breasts and her mass of pubic hair. She enjoyed the unkempt nakedness of her own body, freed from the smart work uniform. She put the ceiling fan on a low setting, throwing herself gently on the bed and letting the movement of the air above her caress her body. She closed her eyes and listened to the sounds of the street outside as they rose in the warm afternoon air and came muffled through the shutters. She gently stroked herself between her legs until sleep enveloped her.

She did not hear him come into the room, so deep was her sleep. Her eyes opened to see him standing above her, tall and handsome, just as she had remembered. He was wearing his *jellabiya*, the Sudanese version of the *thobe*, the loose, white clothing that enveloped every Arab man. There was an old Arab proverb that she remembered: 'Eat whatever you like, but dress as others do.' That was part of the attraction for her – the unknown, unseen body beneath the all-encompassing neutral robes. The *thobe* (or *thawb* as her Arabic professor had insisted on calling it, though she had heard it called a *dishdasha* on her travels) covered almost everything. Kati could see nothing of his arms as long sleeves enveloped them and only his ankles were visible at the bottom, the fabric not touching the ground so that his robe remained free from *nagâssah*, or impurity.

Nothing was said. Her hand reached out for the cool white cotton cloth and she felt his body beneath it. His thighs were strong, firm, rooting him to the spot as he stood looking down on her. As she looked up to him from the pillow, he seemed to tower above her. Her hands felt for him through the cloth and she saw a movement through the cotton as he became aroused. She reached down and found the hem of his robe, reaching inside it to find his calves and thighs. Still nothing was said and still he did not move. She crept from the bed and onto the floor, lifting his hem until she disappeared inside his *thobe*.

For a moment she felt like a child inside a tent or one of the improvised wigwams that her father used to make for her from garden canes and old sheets. Then she looked up and saw the shadow of his body above her. The coolness of the cloth around her made his flesh feel even hotter. His fingers stroked her back as she caressed him with her tongue. One hand pushed through his thighs to grab his buttocks and pull him closer towards her. Kati was sweating now as she enjoyed him, the heat of the city pressing in on her, his robe caressing her buttocks and thighs as she became more urgent. She heard him gasp as he came and she sank to the floor, his robe still around her. They were still for a moment and then he swept away from her, bent down, lifted her in his arms and threw her onto the bed. 'So much better than a stopover in Hong Kong,' she thought as he lay down beside her. As she dozed, she heard him leave. Heathrow seemed an age away.

It was at the Meridien that she had first had sex with Atif, back in the days when she was doing her volunteer work. Then it was safe and anonymous and so full of international goings-on that anything was possible within its impartial walls. She guessed that sex was the least of it. Arms deals, espionage, who knows what went on there. Now that she used it for work and her crew colleagues were there too, it did not have the glamour that it once had to a twenty-one year old student and it was the last place she wanted to be seen with a local by the others on the flight crew, especially Geoffrey. Gossip was a virtual currency amongst the trolley dollies in the sky and she took every precaution not to be any part of it. The Parthenon was different and while nothing went on without Andreas the manager knowing about it, he was always ready to turn a blind eye to any of his guests' indiscretions. That was what made his hotel such a success; that and the fact that he and his staff could sort out anything for you, wafting you through the bureaucracy and the petty irritations of Sudanese officialdom. Perhaps being Greek was the key somehow, one of a people caught in the middle of the Mediterranean between Europe, Africa and the East with the patient resignation bred of having seen so many civilisations come and go.

It was late by the time she woke and for a moment she wondered where she was. She lay on the bed looking up at the ceiling fan as it slowly whooped around above her. The fan was more a decoration than a cooling device and as she had not switched the air conditioning back on the room was stiflingly hot. Gradually she focused her thoughts and remembered where she was. The slats of the shutters on the window threw long striped shadows on the wall. She noticed a gecko still and patient in a corner eyeing an unsuspecting fly. She was back in Africa, in the middle of Sudan where the Blue Nile met the White Nile in that 'longest kiss in history'. She loved that phrase and lazily wondered who had made it up. One of her professors at SOAS would have known. Here she was where not just the Niles met to join and flow down to Cairo and the Mediterranean, but where Arab Africa and Black Africa met as well. She had studied enough politics to know that the meeting of such different cultures had been the cause of the war that had torn the country to pieces over three long decades. That much she had picked up from her classes as a student, but all the rest, her real knowledge of the Sudan, she had learned during her volunteer work here. As she lay in the calm of her hotel room it was hard to believe that there was a war on, but she had glimpsed the refugee camps that she knew so well on the way in to town and they were evidence of another world beyond the hotel. She was anxious to get back to them to see the young people she had once worked with and above all to see Charlie.

She had a full day off tomorrow. It was a long stopover till a return flight in the early hours of the morning, and she was going to make the most of it. While the others mooched around and went to buy souvenirs at the vast *Souk Arabi* or indulged in the pool and spa at the hotel, she would hire a car and drive through the camps to meet her friends and then out to the edge of desert and see how far she could get before she had to return. It was Monday, virtually the middle of the Muslim week. Had it been Friday she might have thought of going to see the Whirling Dervishes at the Green Mosque, one of her favourite sights in all the world and something that never ceased to give her pleasure. There was, however, another thought in her head as she planned the day.

She had heard that the Nuba, people displaced from their mountain home seven hundred miles to the south of Khartoum, had begun to keep alive the traditions of their famous wrestling matches in the camps. She knew about the wrestling from the tattered postcard she had kept since university days of a wrestler – black, glistening and beautiful sitting in triumph on the shoulders of another. It had always been on her desk through college and became an icon of everything she imagined Africa to be, long before she had ever set foot on the continent.

It was a sexy image, of beautiful male bodies untainted by the West, and was an image that had remained with her ever since. Even now, years later, after so many trips to Africa and seeing it in all its many colours, she still loved that photograph and had it framed by her desk in her flat in west London. The great German photographer Leni Reifenstahl had taken the picture during her African love affair, a love that replaced an earlier affair with Hitler and the Nazis that ended in a bunker in Berlin in 1945. Whatever her politics, Kati admired

Reifenstahl and envied her her life. The photography, the glamour, the travel, the lovers, even her death at a hundred years old in the arms of a lover fifty years her junior. Everyone had to have a heroine and for Kati it was the extraordinarily romantic Leni Reifenstahl.

It was that photograph of the wrestlers that had been a factor in her choosing to go to the Sudan on her first trip. Then it had been far too dangerous to travel out of the city and she never made it to the south and to the Nuba Mountains. Now, it seemed, the wrestlers had come to her. On her last trip she had heard rumours that a large Nuba community had grown up in the camps and that they were keeping the wrestling that so defined their culture alive in Khartoum. For a while they had gathered well out of town every Friday near the *Sita Al Haj Yousef souk*. That was until the authorities got nervous of so many men congregating together in one place and banned the sport. She had longed to see it and asked around on that last visit. No-one would tell her anything definite, just that yes, the wrestling did still happen but it was informal and at a different place and on a different day every week. Perhaps, just perhaps, there might be wrestling tomorrow and if there was she might be able to find it. The possibility of an adventure made her blood tingle and she knew that even if she did not find the wrestlers, searching for them would be an adventure in itself. That would be tomorrow. Tonight she would have supper with Atif.

They ate at a vast restaurant over the bridge from Khartoum proper in Omdurman on the banks of the conjoined Nile and looking out onto Tuti Island. Festoons of coloured lights were all along the road decorating the outsides of the many bustling restaurants. There seemed to be an endless stretch of these restaurants, each seating hundreds inside and with tables and fountains up to the banks of the river. There were a few other couples but all being as discrete as they were, careful not to hold hands or make any physical contact in public. It was late into the evening and cool in the night air. The restaurants were busy, long tables with dozens of people around them of every age. It was mostly large extended families dining in the restaurants sharing from huge collections of food in the middle of the tables. Babies, children, ancient men and women and middle aged couples sharing from vast platters. It was a heart-warming sight and difficult to believe that this was the capital city of a country at war.

Kati and Atif sat by the river away from the main throng of the restaurant, passing themselves off as a married couple. Even though it was chilly now and the bugs were out near the water's edge, they decided to dine outside, as close to the river as possible. As they sat at the little wrought-iron table, its white enamel flaking off from years on the wide open terrace, they could hear the waters of the Nile next to them. They heard it lapping on the muddy bank and the light from the coloured festoons glittered on the water. This was the Nile proper, a few hundred yards downstream of the confluence of the Blue and White Niles just beyond the bridge in the distance. There were a few lights burning over on the island, probably the brick makers minding their kilns as they turned the red soil from the river's banks into bricks and they could see the traffic in the distance crossing the bridges that linked Omdurman to Khartoum. For a country ravaged by war the food was wonderful. Others were eating *kebabs* and *shawarmas* of chicken and lamb, but they decided to go for the fish, beautifully presented with some rice and vegetables, and freshly pressed fruit juice. They spoke in English.

They had met just before Kati had returned to London at the end of her stint as a volunteer. Atif had been a locally employed assistant with Trans World Aid, able to fix anything for them in a way that only a local Arab could. He drove, he sought permits and permissions, he made contacts and he always knew the customs and protocol that were so essential in making life run smoothly in Khartoum. He was young, certainly younger than Kati, and keen, determined to learn English, make friends and find out about life beyond his home. In many ways he had reminded Kati of her younger self and she quickly took him under her wing. When it came time to leave, only a couple of weeks after they had met, it seemed inevitable that they would make love and never see each other again. Then years later there were the flights to Khartoum and they started to meet again with a brief intensity that consumed them both. Atif had done well for himself and was now working for the UNESCO office in Khartoum, helping them as he had helped her charity, but on a bigger salary, with much more prestige, and with the keys to a burnished white Range Rover with the UNESCO emblem in blue on its sides. That was how they had driven out over the bridge to Omdurman. She told him about her life, and for him it was something fantastical and faraway. He told her about his and she understood it all and glowed with pride at his success. One day perhaps, when the war really was over and the borders re-opened, he would be able to travel and visit her in London. Things would be very different if that were ever to happen and the wonder and romance of these brief trysts at the whim of British Airways would disappear in the reality of the difference of both their lives. All that was left unspoken tonight, as on every night of these trips, and with so much else to talk about neither of them thought of the future but relaxed and enjoyed the night, chaperoned by the waters of the Nile.

Afterwards he drove her back to the Meridien, past a group of soldiers smoking cigarettes outside the Presidential Palace nearby, and, unable to kiss, waved as she left him. Though she would slip away and sleep at the Parthenon, she thought it best to return to the official hotel and show her face to the others. It was quiet in the hotel when she got back. Geoffrey was there at one corner of the bar with Chris his number two and the other flight attendants. She had promised to meet them for a drink and it would have been rude not to have shown up.

'Where have you been, may we ask?' Geoff's speech was a little slurred and she doubted he would remember the conversation in the morning. Even so she gave little away.

'Practicing my Arabic,' she replied. 'Any chance of a drink?'

CHAPTER THREE

Khartoum

One last drink and then he would try and doze. The alcohol would help. There would be precious little once he was off the plane, the Islamist government had seen to that. The Sudan was a dry country and once he landed the only chance of a tipple would be in one of the Western embassies or, if he was very lucky and discrete, in the hotel. A regular gin and tonic had become such a part of his routine now, a relaxation at the end of the day back home, that he knew how much he would miss it. So another gin and tonic it was from the trolley as it came down the aisle. There would be time to sleep it off during the long hot afternoon in Khartoum when everything came to a standstill in the unrelenting sun. If he would have to forego the alcohol in Khartoum, at least he would be able to smoke. He would also have the sun. After his last trip to the continent, three or four years ago, he had had trouble reading and doing detailed work in the nursery. 'Your eyes are missing Africa,' his optician had told him when he had gone for a check up. He was returning now to the African sun where everything would become clearer, even the mysteries that surrounded his trip.

The flight was almost empty and he had been able to get a seat by the emergency exit. It was a good omen and a sign that luck was with him, he thought as he stretched out his long frame. He was never comfortable flying, but this was as good as it could get; the Club never sent him in anything better than economy. Still it could be worse, he could be on one of those aid trips he used to have to fly, picked up at Manston airport, a relic of the nineteen-thirties in the fields of Kent close to his home, and sat amidst a pile of emergency provisions to be dropped by parachute along with him in the middle of some God-forsaken region. He often wondered why God had forsaken these places Himself and left Oxfam to do His work on His behalf while He did not seem to have forsaken Alec's little corner of Kent at all. Still, it never did to be too philosophical about these things and Alec left the mysterious ways of God for others to worry about while he concentrated on the job in hand, whatever that job might be. The aid planes were often used as a cover for getting behind the front line or into some of the remotest of regions without the protocol that going through diplomatic channels would have involved. 'We'll Oxfam you in,' the Secretary would say, using a favourite verb. It was years since he had done a trip like that hanging from a parachute next to bags of rice. Now there was nowhere he wanted to travel to for work or duty unless he felt he absolutely had to and for pleasure he need go no further than the greenhouses in the gardens of his estate.

Alec looked around the plane. There was a large family in Muslim dress towards the back of the cabin and just a few other people, all African and Chinese. He was the only European. An attractive stewardess looked through from the first class cabin and they caught each others eyes and smiled across the empty seats. Thinking better of watching a movie and knowing he would need all the sleep he could get, he slid his seat back, closed his eyes and dozed off. The next thing he noticed was a rather over-familiar touch on his shoulder from a steward waking him for breakfast. The congealed scrambled egg and the ice cold croissant did not look very appealing but, not being sure what the food prospects might be once he was in Khartoum, he thought he had better eat what he could. Outside the sun had risen and he could make out the Nile beneath him snaking through the arid landscape. As the breakfast was cleared and Khartoum came into sight he saw the shape of the river dominating the vast city, *Al-Khurtum* – the elephant's trunk in Arabic. He peered through the window to see if he could make out the trunk of the Blue Nile snaking away from the White and conjoined Nile rivers that were supposed to make up the elephant's face but it was no easier than it had been staring at the sky when he was a boy and trying to make out the constellations.

As he left the plane he caught site of the stewardess he had noticed the night before on the flight. She was gorgeous to look at, a female Lawrence of Arabia, legs up to her armpits and flaxen blonde hair. He knew about flax, *Linum usitatissimum,* even grew a little in Kent, and this girl's hair was definitely the colour of the long pale stalks. She said goodbye to him as she did, mechanically, to all the others, but for a moment their eyes met again and they exchanged a smile. Alec did not take it personally. 'She's just doing her job,' he told himself and fumbled for his cigarettes as we walked down the steps and onto the tarmac. He had not had a cigarette since before getting to Heathrow and as he inhaled the smoke hit his throat and lungs like a long lost friend. He stood still and enjoyed the combined pleasures of the sun searing onto his face and the nicotine kicking into his veins, taking a few deep breaths before pulling his old buckskin hat from his bag and putting it on his head where it fitted with the comfort of years of intimate wear.

There was a great flurry as he got off the plane and he let things calm down while he finished the cigarette. A big black car whisked off an important man who must have been sitting in first class. A UN-marked Range Rover took a couple of others off and a battered airport minibus was waiting for him. While the rest of the passengers trudged across the runway, he stubbed his cigarette onto the hot tarmac, got into the minibus and was taken off to be deposited at the terminal by a door with a large VIP sign above it. Things were looking up, he thought, and rather foolishly expected to be waved through and on his way. But then he remembered that he was in both the African and the Arab worlds. In neither did things happen quickly, certainly not things involving officialdom. So while all his fellow passengers lined up to be processed behind the glass, he had his papers taken from him with much ceremony by a short neatly-dressed Arab who claimed to work for the British Council, and was left to wait in the VIP lounge. It was hardly luxurious and was so busy, with people endlessly coming and going, that there seemed to be no apparent discrimination as to who really was a VIP. With a fan slowly turning above him and disturbing the flies as they hung in the sweltering heat, he lit another cigarette.

His minder from the British Council arrived, a man in his early sixties, all in khaki except for a flamboyant pink bandana around his neck.

'Hi, you must be Alec. I'm Donald. Good to meet you. I say, couldn't cadge a fag could I? Thanks awfully. Sorry to be late. Traffic's bloody murder, my dear. You've no idea. Have they dealt with your visa yet? They can take forever, poor loves.

They'll be so excited to have a celebrity to deal with. It's mostly very dull for them.'

Alec could scarcely get a word in. It could not be easy being gay in Sudan, Alec thought. What was it that took people like Donald to postings in these out-of-the-way places where such love dared not speak it's name and where the best he could hope for if caught *in flagrante* was to be reposted while his boyfriend had his hands cut off, or worse. Alec did not know what punishment there was for homosexuality under *Sharia* law, but he was sure that it could not be pleasant – unless, that is, your sexual tastes were so extreme that you enjoyed the punishment. Even for a British official with the protection of the crown it would not do to get caught. No wonder Donald was so jumpy. The heat probably did not help; he constantly dripped with perspiration and wiped his brow with a huge handkerchief even this early in the day. Alec rather welcomed the heat. It was a bit like being back in his nursery greenhouse in Kent on a summer's day.

Donald looked every inch the contemporary colonial. A stained cotton suit, a day or two's growth of pale beard, and endlessly chatty, ever keen to hear news from home. Alec was sure he had met this British Council chap before in Syria, or was it the Ukraine?

'The talk on gardening is all planned,' Donald told him and then whispered, 'it will be a useful cover.'

So Donald was in on the plan. The British Council was always useful. Any country that was reluctant to give out visas to foreigners could be relied upon to have a British Council office that could organise one for a visiting writer, even a gardening writer in the middle of the desert. There was something trustworthy about the Council, as if it was not an arm of diplomacy or politics at all. No matter what trouble there was, with Embassies withdrawing staff or having them withdrawn by host governments, the British Council, like some ancient dowager, carried on regardless. There had been a spot of bother in a Russian office recently, he had heard, a politician's son given a posting as a favour and getting recklessly drunk and shagging the natives, but that was the rare exception. For the most part the Council carried on in the remotest of places, paying its way by selling the English language to young people that would never be granted a visa to visit Britain.

They were interrupted by a reporter from the 'Khartoum Times', keen to interview Alec and take his photograph. He was a thin young fellow, smartly dressed in suit and tie, who seemed in awe of Alec's relationship with the BBC. Alec was keen to get on, anxious not to waste time. He had a busy few days ahead: he had to save the world and give a talk to the assembled ex-pats at the British Council's library, but he answered the young man's questions patiently. Donald was anxious too, more about the talk than the saving the world bit.

At last the interview was over and Alec's passport was returned with great ceremony, its inner pages emblazoned with little stamps, stickers and Arabic scribbles.

'You'll still need to be registered with the police and get a licence for your camera,' Donald told him, 'but we can sort all that out at your hotel. You'll probably be wanting a shower and a rest. It gets bloody hot by midday and nobody does a bugger all afternoon until the sun begins to go and evening prayers are out of the away.'

'What bugger is that?' joked Alec sardonically but the remark was lost on Donald who had disappeared ahead to look for the white Range Rover with its British Council logos splashed on its sides which would bump them into town.

'You'll get a good crowd,' Donald told him once they had retrieved Alec's suitcase and set off. 'It's the British Ambassador's turn to organise a do, so all the other diplomatic staff will pop by to see the visitor from England. We take it in turns. The French 'dos' are the best and the German's know how to put on a spread – though they did get into a pickle with a hog roast on Goethe's birthday.'

Alec could not decide whether he was trying to be funny.

'Will there be gardeners?' he asked.

'You must be joking. You can't grow much of anything here unless you've got one of the villas down on the Nile. Fantastic palaces some of them, for the rich and powerful with their moorings on the river and cascades of greenery. Politicians, mostly, and the secret police have got a big place on the river to make it easy to feed people to the crocodiles. But once you step away from the shore it's all dust and desert.'

'Now you are joking. Surely they don't feed people to crocodiles. This isn't Ancient Egypt.'

'I wouldn't be too sure.'

They left the airport and turned right onto Africa Road. Donald kept talking as he weaved amongst the motorised rickshaws that seemed to be everywhere. 'Most of the embassies and the international clubs are around here. Our embassy and the Council are in town, not far from where you're staying.'

The roads were wide and sandy, only some were tarred and those were badly potholed. It was a bumpy ride and Alec realised that he had forgotten to pack sunglasses for the trip. He might welcome seeing the African sun again but in the bleached white urban landscape with every concrete building reflecting the sun at him, he would be grateful for a pair of shades.

'Don't worry,' Donald reassured him. 'We've got plenty of spare pairs. That and hats. Visitors never realise how bloody sunny it is going to be. Fish around in the glove compartment, there's bound to be a pair in there. Probably some sun screen as well, though you don't look the kind of fellow who uses it.'

Alec did as he was told and found just what he needed.

Donald took them on a scenic route to the hotel, across the railway line and down the expansive *El Mek Nimir Avenue* until there in front of them was the river. 'This is the Blue Nile,' Donald told him, 'just before it meets the White Nile and becomes the Nile proper.' Donald had seen it all a million times but for Alec it was a special moment, to be here at the beginning of the river that he knew so well, thousands of miles away where it reached the sea and Uncle Leo in Cairo. As they turned left to drive along the bank of the river, Donald stopped. 'That's Kitchener's old boat over there.' He pointed to a rusting hulk on the grass. 'It's in the sailing club. Might get a chance to drop by later in the week if things work out. Better not stop though, we're just by the Ministry of Defence.' Alec noticed a backpacker trudging along the road by the boat, conspicuous with his dirty blonde dreads and unkempt hair. Here in one of the most remote areas of the world, about which even Lonely Planet had yet to write a guide, was a backpacker. These people seemed oblivious to borders and got everywhere in search of the loneliest spot and the best smoke. There might be nothing to drink in the Muslim world but there was no shortage of things to smoke. How did they do it, Alec wondered. The backpacker looked so out of place and yet at the same time strangely anonymous, just one of the thousands tramping the globe, indistinguishable the one from the other.

'We'll drive along the river past the Coptic Church and the National Museum so you can get your bearings, then we'll go to the hotel, it's only a couple of blocks back from the river.'

They drove slowly, not a difficult thing to do amidst so much traffic, past little groups of soldiers and policemen keeping the traffic moving. Ahead of them a great metal bridge spanned the river like something out of an industrial city in the north of England. 'It's the Old White Nile Bridge connecting Khartoum which is where we are with Omdurman over the water.'

'Like a bridle on the Elephant's Trunk!'

'So you know the story? Yes, the bridge crosses where the White and Blue Niles meet. Khartoum North is over there.' Donald gestured to the right across the river. 'That's Tuti Island in the middle. Good for bird spotting I'm told. We can stop here and get a cool drink if you like.'

They parked by a stall selling ersatz Coke and Fanta from bottles that had been recycled so often that they looked like something from the time of the Pharaohs. The vendor stabbed straws into the bottles and handed them to Donald in exchange for some equally ancient notes.

Across the water on the island, men were fishing in the water and brick makers were fetching clay from the river bank, fashioning it into blocks and firing them in kilns. Red bricks all of approximately the same size and shape yet all of exactly the same colour were piled everywhere. The river banks were populated by the brick makers, most especially on the island. Men had been working these river banks since human habitation began thousands of years ago. Little if anything had changed in the way they carried out their work, an ancient skill passed down the generations from father to son. Along the length of the Nile this work had been going on from the time of the Pharaohs and beyond.

'Looks Victorian,' said Alec, staring at the bridge once they were back in the Range Rover.

'Yes it is. Wasn't meant for here though. A firm called Dorman Long built it in Middlesbrough and shipped it out to India. Then we changed our mind and brought it all the way here. Kitchener thought it would be more useful in the Sudan than over some river in India so they took it apart girder by girder, shipped it across the Indian Ocean, brought it here and reassembled it. Two thousand and twelve feet long, with seven fixed spans and one swing span in the middle, though that's never used any more. Three thousand, seven hundred tons and it's been shipped all around the world.'

Alec was impressed. 'You've done your homework.'

'Not really, we had a talk on it at the Council the other week.' They were staring out of the window at the bumper to bumper traffic, the three wheeled taxis and the crammed taxi buses. 'It can't take the strain of modern traffic anymore so they have to alternate the flow across the bridge at the busiest times – you can be stuck for hours. Things are a bit easier with the new bridge, but not much.'

Alec had taken out his camera and was about to take a picture when Donald stopped him. 'Careful now! Don't even think of taking a picture without a permit. You'll need a permit for the hotel itself and the staff there will get you the documents you need for your camera. Just say that you're taking pictures of cacti or some such and be very careful what you do photograph. Virtually everything is out of bounds. Especially bridges for some reason.'

They swung around a corner in a cloud of dust and screeched to a stop. 'Here we are,' said Donald. 'Welcome to your Khartoum home.' An old piece of neon that had clearly not been lit up for years spelt out the word 'Parthenon'. 'This is a special place,' Donald told him, though there was nothing about the façade of crumbling concrete to indicate just how special the Parthenon was.

It was getting on for noon by the time they reached the hotel and as he stepped out of the vehicle Alec could feel what Donald meant about the heat. A shady promenade went the length of the street and the entrance to the hotel was a few steps back in the darkness, away from the glaring sunshine. There was a cool marbled hallway with an old man gently sweeping the dust and sand back into the street, a task worthy of Sisyphus, and beyond it a wide stairway up to the foyer of the hotel itself. Apart from the old man with his broom there was nobody about. It was suddenly very quiet.

'Everything stops for prayers here,' said Donald. 'For us English, everything stops for tea. It's a cultural accommodation. They have their prayer mats and we have our McVities digestives. Come up and we'll get them to put on the kettle.'

'We always put people up at the Parthenon,' said Donald as they reached the top of the stairs, 'it's clean, safe, you won't get food poisoning and if you're lucky you might even get a cold beer.'

Up the stairs in the foyer there were a few sofas and chairs around a large, low coffee table, a couple of computers at one side with a sign saying 'Internet Café' stuck to the wall behind them, another wide staircase leading to the next floor, and doors and passageways off every corner.

'Andreas, I've got your guest,' shouted Donald towards the busy office in the corner, a space piled up with boxes and papers and all manner of clutter. The door was wide open and a tall, affable figure emerged from the depths beyond it.

'Welcome, welcome, Mr Alec. You are most welcome to the Parthenon.'

'We try and put all our visitors up here, don't we Andreas?' said Donald. Cups of tea had appeared in front of them as soon as they had sat down. 'It is hibiscus tea, Mr Alec, made from the best Sudanese hibiscus leaves.'

Alec sipped the ruby red liquid. 'Thank you Andreas,' he said.

'I am glad you like it. It is especially popular amongst our American guests. It is impossible to buy it in the United States since the trade embargo and the hibiscus of the Sudan is renowned as the best in the world.'

'*Hibiscus sabdariffa*, I must find some seeds to take back with me to England.'

'Maybe someone could give you some at your talk,' said Donald. 'I prefer PG Tips but you can't get it here.'

They drank their tea while Andreas went off with Alec's passport and dealt with the necessary paperwork. Donald began chatting again. 'It's the only place I'd recommend to be honest. There's no tourist trade here, hasn't been for years, so there are no hotels that cater for western needs, expect for the great Meridian down by the river and you wouldn't want to stay there. Andreas and his wife can organise anything for you. His family have been here for years. His father opened the place in the swinging sixties when Khartoum was the fashionable place to come. I bet your neon sign worked then, eh Andreas?' he shouted towards the office. 'Khartoum was all nightclubs and miniskirts and bathing in bikinis in the Nile. It was quite something until Numayri got into power and blew it all away.'

Andreas returned with a couple of forms to fill out. 'You'll need this one for your camera and this if you want to travel out of town, Mr Alec. Just fill them in and leave the rest to me. Have you got some spare passport photos? Not to worry, I will get some made from the one in your passport – you need them for everything here. And you'll be needing some money. Just let me know how much and we will change it for you. You can use dollars and sterling in many places but it is best to have some Sudanese pounds on you. I will let you have your passport back once we've sent it down to the Alien Department for the paperwork. Best to keep a copy of it on you and leave the original and anything else you value with me in our strongbox. I will have someone take you up to your room.'

'I'll leave you here, dear,' said Donald. 'Catch up on your sleep and we'll rendezvous later. We've organised a driver for you. He'll come to pick you up around six, after evening prayers, and bring you around to the Embassy. There's a decent enough bar there. We can have a drink and make a plan. See you later.' With a flourish of his pink bandana, Donald was off.

An old man in a well-worn robe carried Alec's bags for him up to his room on the next floor, through a spotless dining room, with white table cloths laid on metal tables and smart wooden chairs that must have been new when Andreas's father opened the hotel. Alec's room too was spotless, dominated by a huge low double bed, its sheets neatly turned back. There was a dressing table with a mirror against the wall in front of the bed and an old wicker chair by the window. Alec checked out the spacious shower and toilet which, though old, were as clean as the rest of the suite. There was even a spare toilet roll, always a good sign in this part of the world. The shutters were closed to keep the sun out of the room and an air conditioning unit chugged out cold air. There was a large chipped glass ashtray by the bed and Alec needed no more encouragement. He kicked off his shoes, stretched himself out on the pale worn candlewick bed cover and lit up, blowing smoke rings towards the ceiling and watching as the slowly moving fan dispersed them around the room. What adventures were in store, he wondered, and when would the adventures begin? Realising how dog tired he was and bored with the cigarette, he stubbed it out in the ashtray, set the alarm on his watch and went to sleep.

* * *

Getting up later he showered, dried himself on the thin white towel and dressed in a new pair of flannels and a long-sleeved cream shirt. He gave a quick spray of insect repellent to his ankles and rubbed it on his hands and around his neck and face. The last thing he wanted was to be bitten tonight. Leaving his suitcase on the bed he made sure he had his cigarettes and went down to the reception to wait for his driver.

The foyer at the Parthenon was a hive of activity. Three men were shouting at each other in Arabic, a pretty young American girl was picking out letters on the keyboard of a computer in the 'Internet Café', there were some aid workers chatting animatedly in what might have been Swedish, and a journalist hammering out a story on his laptop. This is where Alec would have preferred to spend the evening, drinking hibiscus tea, listening in on all the gossip from Andreas and his wife or from the journalists and international flotsam and jetsam that seemed to be hanging around the lobby, and just soaking up the atmosphere. He loved nothing better than to slip into the background of a new place and get slowly acquainted to his surroundings. There was, however, work to be done and a cover to be maintained and Donald had decided on spending the evening in one of the few places where there was a drink to be had in Khartoum. Alec knew what these embassy bars were like and prepared himself for an evening of ex-pat and NGO gossip, the usual stuff about who was sleeping with whom. Still, experience had taught him that it was always useful to know the local sleeping arrangements, especially as the new man in town, which would mean, if past experience was anything to go by, he could have his choice tonight and add to the gossip. He sat back in an old leather armchair and smoked a cigarette as he thought about all this until a figure came up the stairs from the street and stood politely in front of him.

'Mr Alec, Sir, I am Gamal, your driver.'

'*Salam*, Gamal, I hope you have a car and are not just a camel to carry me on your back.'

'So, you understand Arabic, Sir? I am indeed Gamal, the camel, but still a son of Adam. Perhaps it was my parents' humour to name me so, or perhaps they knew that one day I would be a driver and carry people where they need to go. I see you are smoking the cigarettes they named after me,' Gamal joked as Alec tucked his packet into the top pocket of his shirt.

Alec stood up and shook Gamal's hand. 'It is a pleasure to meet you my friend. Come, let us go to the Embassy.'

Downstairs in the shade of the flaking stucco was Gamal's

vehicle, a smart white British Council six-seater minibus, parked in the dust.

The Pickwick Bar at the British Embassy was not the most salubrious rendezvous in the world but it did serve alcohol and in the bone dry country of the Sudan that was the rarest of things. It might have been the bar at the Club in London were it not for the heat, and the vast French windows open to a garden of palm trees, a sprinkler swishing in the hot air as it watered the lawn. Alec thought that he could be stepping into any ex-pat bar in a third world country. The usual crowd was there and some of them sounded as if they could have stepped out of the pages of a Dickens' novel. Donald was sitting chatting to the barman and already a little sozzled. He introduced Alec to the others, all on Her Majesty's payroll working for DFID, the UK's Department for International Development, or for the Embassy itself. There was an air of languorous boredom about the place, of people trapped in a far away land with nothing to do and no-one to talk to, of no new conversations left to have. The drinks were served with a colonial elegance that Alec had thought to have disappeared decades before. The men eyed him shiftily and the women stared at him with scarcely concealed lust. He was the new man in town and the delicate balance of sexual forces within the ex-pat community was thrown into disarray. His presence had done more to disturb the air than the large dust-encrusted fan that chugged around on the ceiling in the middle of the room.

A young man working for DFID was moaning about the difficulties of getting all his belongings to Khartoum for his stint here. He had been in Sudan for a month already and still most of his effects were back in the UK.

'They were meant to be shipping my piano out weeks ago

but it still hasn't arrived. Not a lot to ask is it if they expect you to work in this god-forsaken dump?'

Many were only too happy to echo his complaints.

'So do they ship everything out?' Alec asked.

'Just the first thousand kg. After that they expect you to pay for it yourself.'

'A thousand kilograms?' Alec was astonished. 'That seems rather a lot.'

'Hardly,' the young man replied, 'and the big stuff has to be sent by sea. Have you any idea how long it takes to get something to the middle of Africa without putting it on an airplane?'

Alec thought it better not to get drawn into an argument about the rights and wrongs of shipping civil servants' households to some of the poorest places on earth.

He and Donald made idle conversation until Donald's bladder got the better of him and he toddled off to the toilet. Alec swirled his ice in the glass and then felt a conspiratorial whisper in his ear. 'My husband's good for nothing,' said a voice and he turned to see a woman in her sixties as brown and dry from the sun as a fossilised raisin taking advantage of Donald's absence. 'I'm Dolly. You really must come and visit us. You can bring your seeds and I'll let you play with my dibber. You'd be surprised at the things we get up to to keep ourselves amused out here. If it gets too exhausting you'll find a little lie down out of the afternoon heat will be a real relief. The heat can be stifling.' Alec swallowed hard, muttered something and stared at the toilet door waiting for Donald to re-emerge. 'Now don't play hard to get will you. I don't want you going off to one of the other Embassies, that would never do. Oh hello Donald, cruising the lavs were we?'

'Hello Dolly,' replied Donald and turned to Alec. 'I see you've already met the Ambassador's wife.'

Dolly tottered off but not before she'd left a large red impression from her lips on Alec's cheek. 'You know where to find me!' were her parting words.

By the end of the evening Alec had exhausted his powers of small talk and was glad to get a few moments of quiet before going back to the hotel. Still his cover was in place and he had a full day before his talk at the British Council, and more importantly the *Moulid,* to get his job done. He and Donald began to make plans for the following day when there was a sudden commotion at the door and all heads turned to see what was causing the excitement. A large, ruddy face man in his late thirties had burst into the bar in a khaki safari suit. A member of the embassy staff was stumbling behind him struggling with bags and cases.

'I say, any chance of a drink, this thing's nearly empty,' said the figure, waving a hip flask in the air.

'David!' Alec exclaimed, 'what the devil are you doing here?'

'The Secretary asked me to drop by in case I could be any help. I was down in Kenya sorting out a spot of bother, so was the nearest member. I got a call a few days ago to see if I could get up here and lend a hand.'

'It's good to see you.'

'You too old man. Always happy to help.'

Alec made the introductions and then Donald went to order some drinks.

'How did you get here?' Alec asked.

'By taxi.'

'From the airport?'

'No, from Kenya. I picked one up the other side of the border and just kept heading north. Terribly nice driver, guy called David which is a bit of a coincidence. He's never been to Sudan before.'

'You mean he's with you.'

'Yes, downstairs, taking a kip in his cab. Must be tired after the drive. It's a bloody long way, I can tell you. Further than I expected.'

'I should say it's a bloody long way.' Donald looked amazed. 'It must be a thousand miles. And the roads are impassable, either washed away in the rains, pot holed, mined or covered with SLA checkpoints. How on earth did you manage it?'

'Well, it was down to David really. He did the driving. I just kept my head down and he kept the meter running. I owe him a few bob by now I dare say.'

It seemed impossible, to have driven all the way from Kenya even in an armoured vehicle, let alone in a taxi.

'How did you get across the border?' Alec wanted to know.

'Bit of baksheesh and lots of shouting. The Kenyans weren't bothered about me going out and the guards on the Sudanese side were just kids really and David didn't take any nonsense from them.'

'Shouldn't we bring him in for something to eat?'

'I shouldn't worry. He'll be fine. He's not too keen on leaving the cab to be honest.'

'What about his family? Won't his wife be worried?'

'I don't see why. Mine isn't. Have you got a ciggie? I'm gasping for one.'

'Just Camel filters.'

'Perfect, better than these African things I've been smoking.'

They strolled into the garden with their cigarettes, leaving Donald to deal with the bags.

'So what's this all about? Something really nasty I'm guessing, to have winkled you away from your geraniums.'

Alec filled him in as best he could and told him of his meetings with André and the minister in London and of his evening in the Pickwick Bar.

Once the last guests had gone, the three of them sat in the corner of the bar to decide on a plan. Donald began, as if setting out an agenda at some British Council meeting. He outlined everything that Alec had been told at the Club and at the Foreign Office. Donald recounted the talk of oil and religion, said about the fears of a plot and a possible explosion and of taking control of oil supplies or disrupting them. Islamist extremists were unhappy with the increasing moderation of a regime in the Sudan that was unable to impose *Sharia* law in the biggest country in Africa and that might be where the new *Mahdi* came into the picture. There was a dream of an Islamic nation spreading from Iran, through Iraq across the Gulf to Somalia, Sudan and once in Sudan down into Sub-Saharan Africa. Sudan was the biggest piece of that jigsaw. The theory was that something was planned for the birthday of The Prophet that would be the most spectacular birthday present imaginable. But what and where? They had perhaps forty-eight hours to find out.

'It's all a bit thin,' thought David. 'It's no more than spooks' gossip. Just rumours.'

'He's right,' agreed Alec. 'It's really not much to go on.'

'It's the best we can do. We're sure that something is planned to happen during the celebrations of The Prophet's birthday this week and we are pretty sure that whoever is planning it is somewhere here in Khartoum and hiding out in the Displaced Persons Camps.'

'What are they?' David wanted to know.

'They're refugee camps really but they can't be called that,' Donald explained, 'because the people in them haven't left the country. If they had crossed a border they could be official refugees and have status with the UN and all the rest of it. But they've just moved from one part of Sudan to another, and until they get the independence they are fighting for, their homes down south are part of Sudan. So they are officially just 'displaced' until they choose to go home. They are refugee camps in all but name and have grown up over decades since the fighting began. People reckon if they can get as far as Khartoum they'll have some sort of safety. And that's pretty much true. Life is basic. Some of the NGOs have been allowed to go in, but the military keep a lid on it all and, if there's a whiff of trouble, come down hard.'

'It's not much to go on is it?' David observed. 'Just some vague talk of a plot being hatched in the middle of millions of refugees.'

'It's all we've got, I'm afraid. We're lucky to have that much. And we do know that it's set for the weekend of The Prophet's birthday so there's a time-frame for us.'

'You and your British Council speak. We need more than a frigging time frame,' David exploded. 'What are we supposed to do, just potter off around the camps like tourists hoping to spot something unusual? Popping our heads around people's doors and asking if they've seen anything suspicious? Alec can get away with it. He'll pass as a native but you don't expect me to tog up like a bloody Arab? I don't speak the lingo for a start.'

Alec intervened. He knew David was not the buffoon he

was making himself out to be and that the buffoonery was his best disguise. He might not speak any Arabic but his knowledge of the Bantu languages of southern Africa were first rate and he had an easy-going way with the Africans that brought him respect wherever he went. What was more he had the heart of a lion and was the best person to have around if things got tricky. He may have seemed a fool but he was the bravest, shrewdest friend you could wish for in a tight corner.

'Don't let him get to you, David. You've got your NGO contacts and you've got your black languages. It will make complete sense for someone like you to be going around the camps asking questions and it'll take the heat off of me if anyone is looking out for intruders.'

David calmed down. 'You're right. Good idea. Sorry chaps, it's been a long drive.'

'So who can help us in the camps? I guess you're not expecting us to just go off on our own are you? Do we have contacts there?' Alec asked.

'We don't but you do, Alec. A friend of yours is working there. Frank Sheridan?'

'Father Frankie? You must be joking?'

'No, the brothers put him in there a couple of years ago as soon as the government let them. He's doing a great job by all accounts.'

'How do we get hold of him?'

'I got a message through to him earlier in the week. He'll be expecting you. Just don't do anything to compromise him. He's a useful pair of eyes and ears for us but he's fiercely independent.'

'You bet he is. He's not one to take sides.'

'Typical bloody Anglican,' grumbled David.

'He's a Catholic actually,' Alec corrected him. 'So he'll be my first port of call tomorrow. What about you David?'

'Like you said, I think I might just go for a drive. Take the focus off you. I can be the white man in the desert. I'll say I'm doing a bit of research for DFID, you know, seeing how our money's being spent. I guess not all of it is going on shipping pianos around the world.' Alec had told him about the young man he had met earlier in the evening. 'Some of it must get to the people who need it. Everyone will be so busy admiring me that they'll never notice you if you're togged up in your Arab gear. I can be your decoy. I might even be able to suss something out, you never know.'

'Perfect,' said Donald, bringing the meeting to a close, 'We'd better get into the Embassy to check that your visas and things are all OK.'

'What about the authorities? Does anyone know we're here? Do they have a clue as to what is going on?' asked Alec.

'We don't know what they know.' Donald answered. 'Though they must know something. Telephones, the internet, everything is monitored and at the whisper of trouble the lines are cut. Even at the Council we can go for days without internet access or decent telephones. So I'd be surprised if they haven't some idea. This is a sophisticated country and the years of war have added to the sophistication. My guess is they won't interfere; they've got enough troubles as it is. But they certainly won't help out. You're on your own here.'

They had talked long into the night. There was time though for a final night cap and a last draw on the cigars David had found in his battered briefcase.

Alec elected to walk back to the hotel and told Gamal to come for him in the morning. 'Where are you staying David?' he asked.

'Don't worry about me, I'll be put up here in the Embassy.'

'And the other David?'

'Oh, he'll sleep in his car, he prefers it that way. See you at your place for breakfast.'

They sauntered out into the night and Donald went off in his Range Rover.

Alec waved him goodbye then gazed up at the stars. A cloud of heavenly bodies brighter than anything Alec could see in Kent. He was close to the river and though it was in the opposite direction to the hotel he walked down to see the Niles languidly moving in front of him. The confluence of the Blue Nile and the White was away in the distance in the dark, the White Nile flowing down from somewhere in the Nyungare Forest in Rwanda a thousand miles away, through Tanzania to Lake Victoria and then through Uganda, the other Blue Nile from Lake Tana in Ethiopia another thousand miles away. Both were joining here in Khartoum for their shared journey through the desert to the Mediterranean and Uncle Leo three thousand miles away. It was a romantic spot and in the quiet of a Khartoum night, with only the water and the stars for company, the history of the place was palpable and the problems of the twenty first century seemed as distant as Cleopatra. For a moment he glimpsed eternity in the flow of the Nile.

They had planned to set off early and so Alec turned reluctantly back to walk the few blocks to the hotel for a full night's sleep before driving out as soon as the day was light.

CHAPTER FOUR

The Camps

Alec was later for breakfast than he would have liked but it was good to have had a solid night's sleep. It might be a while before he would get another one, and he'd enjoyed the coolness of the room and the buzz of the air-conditioning. Now at breakfast he could already feel the heat of the day and he knew it would hit him as soon as he stepped outside. Breakfast at these hotels always seemed to involve eggs. The waiter appeared magically at Alec's side with coffee and toast. The boiled egg was already sitting there hard as a rock on his plate. There was a little buffet with fresh fruit and juices and triangles of Laughing Cow cheese. As he ate, he took time to look around at the other guests. There was a group of what he took to be American NGO workers at one table and at another in the far corner of the room were a couple of Chinese eating in silence. He thought that they might be oil men or engineers. The Chinese were quietly buying up Africa while no-one was watching, building roads and railways in exchange for oil and minerals, just like the colonial powers had done in the scramble for Africa a century ago. A woman was sitting on her own in the far corner, with a copy of what he supposed to be a bible open on the table in front of her, peering at its double columns of close type, with faded red stain on the page ends, and a well worn black leather cover, as she drank her tea. She looked familiar and then Alec remembered having seen her getting off the plane in front of him. The woman looked up at him and Alec buried himself in the 'Khartoum Times' to avoid her attention. There was a picture of himself in the paper with the interview that he had given to the young journalist at the airport. 'Mr Alecs, esteemed gardener', was in Sudan to give a talk. He had one more cup of coffee, the European coffee of Andreas's hotel, not the thick, sweet cardamom flavoured coffee of the Sudan, and then made a move, folding the few thin pages of the newspaper together and sliding them into his pocket as he got up from the table. Back at home he knew that Albert would be proud as punch to read the piece and add it to the scrapbook of press cuttings he collected from his master's trips.

He went downstairs to see if David or his driver had arrived. A tall, slim, blonde girl was leaving down the hotel steps, pulling an old hat over her tightly tied-back hair as she went. Alec watched her go for a moment until a shrill English voice disrupted the calm that the hotel was famous for. A girl with alarmingly ginger hair and a complexion to match was shouting orders to all and sundry. It soon became clear to Alec that she was a journalist from the BBC, in Sudan to report on the trouble in Darfur. The cost of her equipment alone could have fed a refugee camp for months. She had an entourage with her of what Alec took to be a producer and cameraman, the latter a tall, sanguine Frenchman in tee shirt and jeans who shrugged his shoulders a lot and sat on his camera cases rolling a cigarette, lapsing back into French every time the shrillness of the journalist got too much for him. She bossed and fussed around, shouting to

Andreas about permits and visas and cars, to her cameraman about his equipment and to her producer about her hair. If only she had been from the World Service, Alec wished to himself, then she would have been a discrete presence and a possible source of support. Instead she was just another annoying news reporter treating the world as something to build a career on.

The 'crisis' in Darfur as it was known in the media had come up on the Western radar again with some new UN resolution and the BBC must have decided to send someone over. As she blustered around and complained about deadlines not being met, Alec wondered if she had ever been to Africa before. He did not want to be recognised or get caught in conversation so made his way downstairs to the foyer to wait for David, passing the pretty American girl who was still tapping away in the 'Internet Café' on a battered PC that she optimistically hoped would connect her via cyberspace to her family the other side of the world.

As he got to the stairs Alec heard David coming, shouting back at his driver not to leave the car as he came up the steps. Even with a hangover David's face was beaming with anticipation at the day ahead as he trotted up the stairs.

'Have we got time for a coffee?' David asked. 'I overslept and missed breakfast at the Embassy.'

'You get yourself a drink while I load up some water in the cars,' replied Alec.

'Good idea!' David grinned and pottered off to find himself a coffee. One of the hotel staff helped Alec with the bottles of water, tightly wrapped in shrink wrap plastic and covered in Arabic script. Only the 'use by' advice was in English. They would need that water. It was going to be bloody hot today. Alec did not need a weather forecast to tell him that.

Gamal was downstairs waiting for him, sitting patiently crossed-legged in the shade not far from the minibus. He jumped up as soon as he saw Alec.

'Good morning Mr Alec. How are you today?'

'*Sabah el kheer*, Gamal,' said Alec, as keen to practise his Arabic as Gamal was to try out his English. '*Kaifa holoka*?'

'I am very well this morning. How are you?'

'*Ana bekhair, shokran*,' Alec told him.

They tucked the water down behind the driving seats. The bottles were ice cold now but would be warm in minutes once they had set off. There were a few other provisions to keep them going – biscuits, some dry bread, a few bananas, and a little cardboard box of boiled eggs.

He went back to find David and collected his passport from Andreas, filled with yet more stamps and an impressive A4 sheet with his photo attached to it that was his permit to use his camera. He was off to photograph cacti and succulents. At least that was what it said on the permit. David was in the corner flirting with the girl on the computer, though you never knew with David whether he was flirting or just being friendly. Alec guessed that was part of his charm and why he seemed to have no trouble getting women into bed and why they never seemed upset when he disappeared from their lives the morning after.

Alec left David to his flirtation for a few minutes more while he went back to his room to pick up his Arab gear that he had packed neatly into a small rucksack. For the moment he would be Alec Harvey on a field trip for desert plants; the disguise might be useful later.

While he went off in search of indigenous plant life, David would be driving into the camps, a professor of Development Studies (which indeed he was in one of his many lives) acting on behalf of Her Majesty's Government to see for himself what a difference the donations of the British tax payer were making to the lives of the refugees.

Returning to the foyer Alec pulled David away from the attractive girl at the computer and took him downstairs. His driver, the other David, had dozed off in the car, exhausted no doubt from the days of driving and from having to sleep in his car. David prodded him awake.

'Wakey, wakey David, we're off!'

David the driver sat bolt upright at the steering wheel. 'Ready when you are Mr David.'

'Good man. So remind me what the plan is Alec, let's just run through it one more time?'

Just as he was about to reply, Alec noticed the hippy that he had seen by Kitchener's boat yesterday, walking past them and into the hotel. Instinct told him something was not right, but there was no time to do anything about it now. Instead he took David by the arm and walked a few yards down the street in the shade of the veranda, offering him a cigarette as he did so. They went over things as they smoked.

'I'm off to find Father Frankie. Donald has arranged a rendezvous at his church over in Omdurman. From there we'll be able to cover Khartoum North as well. That leaves Khartoum proper for you. You can make your own way around, playing the blundering colonial, and hope you turn something up.'

'Don't worry, I know the drill: "look like the innocent flower but be the serpent under it." '

'Something like that.'

'And I've got a couple of old university mates I can hook up with who are reporting on a new NGO project. Just hope I can find them. Still we've got this far, haven't we Driver David?' They were back at the cars now. 'I'm pretty sure we can handle the last few miles.'

'It's not going to be easy to communicate. There's a chance that the cell phones Donald gave us last night might work but we can't rely on them and even if they do work they'll probably be intercepted. If we can't get hold of each other and the worst happens we'll just have to try and get a message to Donald somehow. Gamal is utterly reliable and knows the camps inside out, he's been driving for the Council for years. You'll have to use your ignorance as a cover to allow you to stop somewhere and ask for help.'

'Okay old man. See you back here later.'

'Yes, here at the hotel after evening prayers.'

They shook hands rather formally knowing that for all their apparent casualness there was a lot at stake.

Gamal, his Sancho Panza, was waiting in the minibus. He got out quietly before they set off and put his trust in Allah, blessing the driving seat with a prayer and a mark on it from his fingers. The air-conditioning rattled into life when Gamal switched on the engine but Alec preferred the windows open, even with the sand blowing up from the road. They would start over the river in the camps outside of Omdurman and drove off through the packed streets the few blocks to the bridge. A handful of military police were hanging around but Alec had tucked his camera away in his rucksack. They were not stopped. Soon they were on the old bridge, brought by the British from India a century and a half ago. It took a while to cross. A yellow taxi had a flat tyre on the rusting ironwork above the Nile and the driver was busy changing the wheel, the passengers resigned to waiting in the heat that burst so many tyres on the sticky tarmac.

'It happens all the time,' Gamal told him. 'But you are not to worry Mr Alec, I have two spare tyres in the boot, and a repair kit, and a very good pump. We will not get into any problems, *Insh'Allah*.'

'Hada shay'un Jameel,' said Alec expressing his relief.

Two lanes of traffic passed in the opposite direction hooting and shouting as they went by the stopped taxi. If there were rules to driving in Khartoum Alec could not work out what they were, but he knew that Gamal would cope with any traffic, calm and impassive no matter what happened. The taxi's tyre was quickly changed and they were on their way again.

They drove through Omdurman past the *souk* and into the camps. It was here that the answer lay and if anyone could point them in the right direction it was Father Frankie. The traffic thinned as they moved out of town and the tarred roads came to an end. Gamal clearly knew where he was going and sped along. Huge palm trees lined the edges of the road and they went past some beautiful houses set back from the traffic behind high walls. Once they hit the edge of town they were on a wide two-lane road, on one side of which was a tract of waste land between the road and the city but on the other side the camps started right up against the road's edge. They passed a petrol station and a supermarket and it was then that Gamal twisted the steering wheel to his left and veered off the road and into the camps. Alec had expected something very different from what at first he found. He had imagined improvised tents and shacks, World Food Programme marquees and queues for food. What he saw was a vast extended urban landscape of buildings sturdily built of brick and mud. Gamal explained that it was a succession of interrelated villages and towns, many of which had been built up over the decades of warfare. Some of the areas were densely packed together with shops and traders established amongst the mud brick buildings and there it was almost impossible to drive through the narrow streets and the deeply rutted, dried mud roads. Other areas were more spacious and spread out. It was a world that seemed to have been baked out of the earth it grew from, a reddish brown townscape scooped and moulded as if by a giant hand out of the soil and sand. Alec marvelled at the human resilience that could make and sustain an urban life in such harsh and unforgiving circumstances.

Gamal sped through the camps, with a seeming second sense to the dangers of the surfaces he was driving along. Alec was completely disorientated. It seemed impossible to him that anyone could have a sense of direction here, with the sun high over head and the monotonous colour of the buildings, all a single storey high, coming to just above the height of the top of their truck. The camps went on forever, stretched along the flat landscape as far as the horizon. He asked Gamal how many people lived here. No-one knew, he was told. It was anybody's guess. Some thought as many as three million, driven from the African south of the country to the Arab north by the civil war that had raged for thirty years. There was a sophisticated infrastructure here amongst the shacks and huts with hardened mud roads, shops, and even electricity in some places close to the city. Alec saw poverty but he also witnessed a pride in the squalor. There was no running water, Gamal told him and Alec saw boys pulling oil drums full of water on donkey carts and selling precious mouthfuls just a mile or two from the greatest river in the world. Alec gulped guiltily on his plastic bottle of mineral water as the sand caught the back of his throat. There was something obscene about being able to buy dozens of bottles of mineral water in a land where children were without anything clean to drink.

After an hour of driving they were further out towards the edges of the camps where the buildings were now shacks and the infrastructure had long disappeared. Gamal drove up to a building larger than those around it at one side of a parched square. A large metal cross made of aluminium pipes towered above it, twenty or thirty foot high and the tallest structure for miles. There were houses around, shacks of mud and cardboard, much less substantial than the ones they had seen closer into town. 'We're here,' said Gamal as he honked on the horn and expertly parked against the side of the church in the tiny amount of shade that it afforded. Alec jumped out and Gamal clambered over his seat and followed him. The familiar towering figure of Father Frankie, six foot four, well built, in his late fifties, dressed in a long black cassock and wearing a dog collar in all this heat, hurried around from behind his church. Only the wide brimmed flat straw hat acted as any concession to his being in Africa.

'I like the hat, Father,' Alec called out.

'The King of the Swazis gave it me. Welcome my boy, it's good to see you. It's been a while.'

'Too long, Father.'

'Welcome to the parish. Hello Gamal, good to see you too.'

Alec hugged his old friend. They had not seen each other for years, not since they were both working in South Africa, and he did not like to think how long ago that had been.

'It's so good to see you. I had no idea you were here. I thought you were still in Nairobi. How have you ended up here of all places?'

'I go wherever I'm needed. An old Irish priest with nowhere to retire to moving around the continent at the whim of the Pope.'

Father Frankie had spent his life in Africa, coming out as a missionary straight from the seminary and never going back.

'There aren't many of us who know this place well enough to be shuttled around like I am. There's always somewhere new to go. The entire continent is on the move. Wars, famine, poverty. Nothing is stable and people spend their lives walking the continent in search of a better life. New parishes spring up suddenly in Africa out of nowhere. You've seen how it is around Cape Town with the squatter camps. Well it's the same up here. Ten years ago where we're standing was barren desert with not a human in sight; now it's some of the most densely packed habitation you'll find anywhere on earth. They don't bring their pastors with them and so the church has to answer a need wherever it sees one.'

'Are you here on you own?' Alec wanted to know.

'No, there are a couple more of us. Two black priests from the south. We cover all of the camps between us, here and Khartoum North and Khartoum itself of course. They stretch around all three of the cities. I don't like to think how many parishioners we must have between us or how many miles we must drive every day. You've no idea how many communion wafers we can get through on a busy week. It can be the only solid food a few of them get some days. Khartoum is encircled by Catholics. It's not a Muslim city at all if you think about it.'

'It's a bit of a change from Nairobi.'

'Oh, I don't know. The job is the same wherever you are in Africa. And I've got a grasp of the black languages of the south, they're not a million miles from the ones in Kenya, so that helps and was one of the reasons they sent me here. There's poverty and spiritual need wherever you go.'

'And the authorities don't mind a Catholic priest being at large here?'

'It's much easier than you'd think. With so many millions living here side by side and such a mix of religions they have to take a pretty *laissez-faire* attitude. It's not just Muslims and Christians, there are lots of traditional beliefs as well brought up here from the south. It's in everybody's interests to somehow make things work and not bring the war into the city. There are the aid groups too, and the NGOs, and foreign governments as well as the churches, and we just all have to find a way of working together and not upsetting each other or the government.'

The priest and the gardener stood and chatted in the sun. Father Sheridan was as much a social worker as a priest and the churches that he ministered in were community centres as much as they were places of worship. They were schools, meeting halls, health centres, places you could come for communion, to learn French or English, have a vaccination, settle disputes, sing and dance or just shoot the breeze with family and friends.

'What brings you to this part of the world? Don't tell me you're giving one of your gardening lectures.'

'As a matter of fact I am,' Alec smiled.

'And I'm the *Mahdi*! Let me make you a coffee and you can tell me all about it. We've got instant – Nescafé – it's much prized here over the fresh ground variety, a real status symbol.'

They went inside the church and the priest lit a little camping stove and filled a kettle from a grubby jerry can.

'It'll be fine if we boil it for a few minutes,' the priest

reassured him. He brought out a tin of coffee powder from somewhere inside his cassock and spooned it into a couple of tin mugs. 'I can't get through the day without copious amounts of the stuff, so I like to keep a little with me on my travels,' he confided. 'Will you have one, Gamal?'

'Yes please Father. Three sugars.'

'This business of a new *Mahdi*,' Alec began once Father Frankie had made the coffee. Alec told him everything he had learnt in London and the previous night at the bar. 'That's all I know. Not much to go on. Have you heard anything? Donald at the British Council said you were keeping your ears open. I guess if this guy is fomenting trouble and raising a rebel army here in the camps he'd have to be bloody clever. Surely people would notice an Arab amongst all these Africans.'

'Not necessarily. The camps are vast and there are many different tribes here, not just from the south. There are Nuba people from the Nuba mountains, displaced Arabs from Darfur, it's not a simple African versus Arab thing at all any more. This is the biggest country in Africa, some say you can find the whole of Africa in Sudan and you can find all of Sudan in the camps of Khartoum. There are millions of people here Alec, from all over, distinct communities with their own ways of life, own customs, beliefs and traditions, keeping themselves to themselves. There are churches everywhere. You've probably noticed them as you drove through, though you might miss some of them I guess, not all have got crosses as wonderful as ours. It was a major job getting hold of the metal and tools to make it I can tell you. Yes, churches of every denomination. We all know each other though. The tribes have got different ways of celebrating mass. They provide all the singing and dancing and I provide the incense and a sermon or two if they need one.

Catholics, Protestants, Methodists, evangelicals, you name it. We're a model of inter-faith tolerance and exchange, and we pop in and out of each others churches all the time.'

'You Catholics have always been good at adapting to the cultures and religions you find wherever you go, haven't you?'

'You have to be tolerant. The days of scaring the poor buggers to death with fire and brimstone are over. These people have been through hell already and know what it's like.'

'You scare them with your driving,' said Gamal. 'I've seen you.'

'You're right my son, but with just three of us and such a giant parish it's often twenty miles between communions. If I dawdled I'd never get through all my wafers, now would I?'

'The war's pretty well over now isn't it? Won't people start going back home?'

'Some maybe, but for many this is the only home they've ever known and they haven't got anywhere to return to. For the blacks this desert in the north is a foreign land but at the same time a land in which their cultures thrive in the dust. It's a difficult journey back south. Some will send one family member first to check things out. Most will want to go one day but not till things are really settled.'

'Can they really think of this as home, Father?' asked Alec looking at the shacks around him.

'They do, many of them, certainly the generations that were born here. The different tribes struggle to keep their customs, traditions and cultures alive here just as they struggle to find food and water. The Kuku, Acholi and Lokoya from Eastern Equatoria, the Dinka and Jur Chol from El Ghazal, the Shilluk and Anywak from Upper Nile, the Bari of Juba, the

Zande from Western Equatoria and the Kwalib from the Nuba mountains of Kordofan, all keep their songs and dances and languages and cultures alive. You could see them later if you like. There's a local group giving a performance at one of the churches.'

'So it's not fanciful to imagine a plot being hatched here hidden amongst all these different communities?'

'Not at all. More coffee?' Father Frankie boiled some more water and made fresh coffee while he talked. 'It would be an ideal place to hide secrets. You could hide anything here and no-one would know. Who would even think to look?'

'We would! But isn't it like looking for a needle in a haystack?'

'Sorry, Mr Alec. What is a haystack?'

Alec explained to Gamal. 'We do not have such an idiom in Arabic because we do not have haystacks. We would say as difficult as paving the sea, or perhaps we should say, like looking for a needle in a sand dune.'

'We've got two big advantages,' the priest continued. 'The first is we know that we are looking for something unusual, something out of place. The second is that we priests are the only people who drive around all of the camps. The NGOs and aid groups and the like just stick to their own patch and on the whole the refugees come to visit them, miles sometimes, for food and water. We priests get to go everywhere, even if we do frighten people with our driving, Gamal.'

'It was merely an observation, Father.'

'You're right, but the Lord watches over me. And while he has been watching over me, I've been watching over the camps, ever since André got a message through to me last week. "Keep your eyes peeled for something unusual," he said.'

'And…?' Alec wanted to know.

'I know just the place to start. At least I think I do. I don't get everywhere myself, but the three of us, me and the other two priests, do get to most places every few weeks. We met up on Sunday after we'd finished all our services. We try and do it every week unless something takes one of us away. That way we can take each others' confessions, give each other communion, and catch up on news and gossip.'

Gamal quietly listened to the talk of strange customs and wondered what communion and confessions were. News and gossip he knew about.

'Surely you can't need confession,' said Alec.

'You'd be surprised my boy. We're none of us pure, isn't that so Gamal? So last Sunday I took the opportunity to ask about new projects, things that might be happening that I'd not heard of, without wanting to give anything away you understand.'

'Did you learn anything?' Alec asked.

'Possibly. There are things happening all the time of course. The camps spread out daily with new shacks and buildings and NGO projects coming in to service them. One of my colleagues, Father Ngubangu, asked if we knew anything about a new church he'd driven past out beyond Mayo in Khartoum North. Neither of us did and that is unusual. Buildings go up quickly here, overnight often, and there are always new churches being built for the new communities that spring up. This was different though. A church without any of us knowing and right out on the edge of the camps beyond any congregation. Father Ngubangu had only seen it in the distance and thought nothing of it until we were talking on Sunday. The more we thought about it though, the stranger it seemed. Not strange that there was a new church, but strange that we knew nothing about it and that it was so isolated. It could be just what you're looking for.'

'Is it likely that an Islamist would use a church as a cover. And what made the Father Ngubangu think it was a church anyway?'

'It had a cross on it. Nothing as ostentatious as ours, but a small wooden one on the roof. That's what made Father Ngubangu notice it.'

'Let's go there then,' said Alec. 'There's no time to be lost, just point us in the right direction.'

'I don't think you should go on your own. If there is something dodgy going on it would be much better that I went ahead of you. I can go anywhere and no-one thinks twice about it. I'm not a visiting white man like you, or a smart Arab like Gamal. This dog collar might be hot, but it's my passport to anywhere. I reckon I'm always going to be conspicuous, let's face it there aren't that many six foot four Irish priests in this part of the world. But I'm part of the landscape. Going into churches is what I do, even if they're not mine.'

'Should we follow you?'

'I tell you what, why don't we go together with Gamal driving. Two vehicles would be conspicuous and Gamal's Arabic might be useful, though yours used to be pretty good if I remember. And it will save me some of my precious petrol if we take your minibus. We'll just need to make a stop or two on the way. I've some parishioners I need to pop in on.'

'Will there be any government troops around?' Alec wanted to know.

'It's unlikely,' said Gamal. 'They don't make regular patrols, just the odd raid if trouble is brewing. We'll be fine with your cover story, and you've got all the right documents.'

'And you Father?' Alec asked.

Father Frankie had rinsed the mugs and packed away the stove. 'Don't worry about me. I've got a dog collar and an Irish passport. We're an oppressed colonial people just like the Sudanese used to be. Oh, and I've got my shellalagh,' he said, reaching for a long heavy stick. 'You can't be too careful of the snakes. ' They walked out through the open entrance of the church and into the sun. Father Frankie folded his large frame into the back of the minibus while Alec and Gamal climbed in in front of him and a cloud of sand was thrown up by their wheels as they drove off.

So the search began. Father Frankie gave directions as they threaded their way through the camps. He had a very sick parishioner that he wanted to see and he had brought with him his ciboria, a worn silver case holding communion wafers. After twenty minutes they stopped at a mud brick house. Gamal decided to stay outside with the vehicle while Alec went inside to watch Father Frankie give communion. It was wonderfully cool inside the house and so dark after the blazing sun outside that it took Alec's eyes a while to adjust and see anything. Not that there was much to see. A few possessions were stacked in a corner and a battered plastic container half full of water was by the door. A rope bed made of sisal on a wooden frame was in the middle of the room, just like the *angareb* Alec had seen his Uncle Leo sleep on in Egypt since he went native. Alec could just make out the shape of a woman lying on it with a sheet drawn over her.

Father Frankie went over and knelt by the figure on the bed, whispering to her and introducing Alec who came over and took the woman's hand. It felt thin and fragile, just dry loose skin over tiny bones. He smiled down at her, thanked her for allowing him into her house, and then stood back by the doorway while Father Frankie said his prayers and gave her communion. She was so frail that he did not even give her a full wafer, but broke a small piece off and lifted her head as she took it on her tongue, bringing out a small plastic bottle of water from his pocket to help her swallow it. Then he laid her head gently back on the floor and ate the rest of the wafer himself. Blessing her and promising to return, he got up and left.

'Sorry Alec, there's me keeping the wafer all to myself, I should have thought to offer you some.'

They carried on driving, Father Frankie getting them to stop every so often when he saw someone he knew, or when someone noticed him and waved them down. They made slow progress as the priest seemed to know everybody. Then it was Gamal who stopped. It was time for him to say his mid-day prayers. Even out here in the camps they could hear the *Athan*, the call to prayer wafting on the warm breezes from the mosques in the city. Gamal got out to pray by the side of the road, taking his prayer mat from the back of the bus. He unrolled it and Alec noticed the large cream coloured plastic compass that was attached to it. Gamal fiddled with the compass until he found the direction of Mecca, swept the ground with his hand to remove any impurities, laid out his mat and got ready to pray.

There was nothing for the others to do but wait.

'I'll just say a few 'Hail Marys',' said the Priest. 'I rarely get the chance to pray for myself these days. Then we can have a spot of lunch.' Father Frankie took out his rosary, the beads running like quicksilver through his fingers as he muttered his prayers to himself, while Alec sat in the shade of the truck with the door open, swung out his legs and lit a cigarette. He watched in fascination as Gamal went through his own ritual.

Out here there was no chance for Gamal to perform any sort of ritual ablution. He stood facing the *Qibla*, the direction of Mecca, his head down, his hands to his side and his feet evenly spaced and Alec heard him expressing his intent to pray. He knew that Gamal could offer as many segments of prayer as he had time for and listened to him intoning in Arabic: 'I intend to offer the four *rakats* of the *Isha* prayer and face the *Qibla* for the sake of Allah and Allah alone.'

Then he began his *Salaa*, his praying, putting the world behind him and standing quietly with respect and attention. He brought his hands to his ears, his palms forward, his thumbs behind earlobes and began to pray: '*Allahu Akbar.*'

God was indeed great, thought Alec, to have these two such different men praying to him in such very different ways. He was not a believer himself but never ceased to wonder at how the most humble and intelligent men he knew had such quiet and strong faiths.

Gamal had now placed his right hand over his left below his navel and was looking at the ground in front of him and reciting aloud the *Fatiha*, the first *surah* of the *Qur'an*.

'In the name of God, the infinitely Compassionate and Merciful. Praise be to God, Lord of all the worlds. The Compassionate, the Merciful. Ruler on the Day of Reckoning. You alone do we worship, and You alone do we ask for help. Guide us on the straight path, the path of those who have received your grace; not the path of those who have brought down wrath, nor of those who wander astray. Amen.'

Would this be a day of reckoning, Alec wondered, as Gamal

dropped his hands to his sides, bent from waist until his back was parallel to the ground put his palms on knees, and continued his prayer.

'Allahu Akbar. Subhanna rabbiyal 'Azeem'

While Father Frankie quietly prayed with his rosary in the shade of the truck, Gamal prostrated himself on the ground, touching his forehead, nose and palms to the mat, and then slowly rose to a sitting position, looking at his lap. He turned up the heel of his right foot, with his right toes bent, prostrated himself again and at last returned to a sitting position, saying *'Allahu Akbar'* as he did so.

Alec knew Gamal was coming to an end as he looked over his right shoulder, towards the angel recording his good deeds and then looked over his left shoulder towards the angel recording all the bad things he had done, saying each time, *'As Salaamu 'alaikum wa rahmatulaah* – Peace and blessings of God be upon you.'

Alec turned away and quietly closed the door of the bus to allow Gamal to say his personal prayers with hands cupped and palms up at chest level. As the priest kissed his rosary and put it away, Gamal wiped his face with his palms, rolled up his mat and returned to the vehicle.

They ate their lunch in silence, each lost in his own thoughts as they snacked on the food Alec had brought from the hotel. The heat and the poverty did little for their appetites. After water and a banana each, they set off again on a journey that was now taking them through some of the most desperate places on God's earth.

'It's a God forsaken place out here,' said Alec as they passed people living in abject poverty.

'God can't have forsaken it if he sends me here, now can he

my boy?' the priest replied and Alec immediately felt humbled by the priest's faith.

Eventually the dwellings began to thin out and the camps came to an end. Beside them was just empty desert. They kept driving through the huts that marked the end of the camps. Father Frankie had been stopping every so often to chat to people and gather snippets of information and told Gamal to stop again when he saw a figure he recognised by the side of the track. Alec sensed that he knew exactly what he was looking for and who might know where to find it. Father Frankie clasped the hands of the old woman he was talking to and climbed back into the bus.

'Keep your eyes peeled. We're nearly there. Circle around the edge of the camps from here Gamal, but try and stay amongst the huts if you can to avoid being seen. The church is somewhere here, a couple of hundred yards or so out into the desert. There's nothing we can do about the dust I'm afraid,' he said as a great cloud spun into the air when they drove off, 'maybe it will help give us some cover if anyone does see us.'

Here on the outskirts of the camps there was just an endless barren vista glimpsed ever so often beyond the huts. Gamal was driving slowly, weaving through the huts and shacks while Alec and the priest scoured the landscape through the gaps between the dwellings. Suddenly Father Frankie told Gamal to stop. He had seen what they were looking for. There in the distance away from the edge of the settlement was the building the Father Ngubangu had talked about. Even Alec could see that something was not right about it. For one thing it was too detached from everything else. 'People build together here, every area is a community,' said Gamal. 'That building is too isolated.'

'You're right, Gamal,' the priest agreed, 'and there are other things. It's not the same shape as every other building and it's not the same size. A building that size could only be a church, but that's definitely not a church.'

'But it has got a cross on it,' said Alec as he peered into the distance and spotted the prominent cross on the building. 'It must be a church.'

'Trust me; I'd know if it was. It just doesn't ring true. Notice how the walls and the roof meet.'

Alec could see nothing unusual.

'There's no gap. The whole building looks completely sealed. All the churches I know, any large building, has a gap between the top of the walls and the roof to let sunlight in and hot air out. And look, there's a door. We would never have a door on one of our churches, there are just entrances through the walls open to all.'

'So why the cross?' asked Alec looking at the structure on the church's roof.

'Let's take a closer look,' said the priest pulling a pair of binoculars from his cassock. Alec wondered what else he kept there; his clothes were like Mary Poppins' carpet bag.

'I'm thinking it could be a disguise. A kind of a catholic camouflage,' said the Priest.

'An Islamist plot inside a Christian church, Father?' asked Gamal.

'Why not, it could be a perfect way to hide something. No-one bothers our churches here in the camps, despite Islamic rule. Oh, they clamp down on our activities once in a while, but for the most part, we are left alone.'

'Or maybe it's more than that,' interrupted Alec, 'take a look.'

Alec had taken the binoculars, focused in on the building and was looking closely at the cross. He passed them to the priest.

'That's not just a cross, it's an aerial and it's not for cell phones. Not way out here.'

'You're right my boy, it is an aerial and I doubt it's to pick up CNN,' said the priest as he peered through the binoculars.

The question now was what to do next. They sat quietly for a while, each lost in his own thoughts. If this was the right place and they had found what they were looking for, something had to be done, and done quickly. There was not time call for reinforcements, no time to go back to Khartoum and make a plan.

Father Frankie broke the silence. 'We don't even know if anyone is in there. Why don't I just go up and find out what's going on? There's nothing strange in priest going into a church.'

They decided this was their best option. Father Frankie would walk to the church and simply go inside, as he would to any other church in the camps, ingenuously enquire what was going on and then report back. Alec and Gamal were to give him thirty minutes. If he did not reappear in that time they would come and find him.

So that's what happened. Alec and Gamal stayed where they were in the bus, hidden behind the shacks and huts. The priest got out of the bus and Alec wished him luck as he left them to walk to the church.

'*Bettawfeeq*, Father Frankie,' said Gamal, echoing Alec.

The priest moved slowly across the sand, his black clothes soaking up the sunlight, and Alec watched him through the binoculars as the door of the church opened and Father Frankie went in.

Alec became anxious very quickly. There must have been someone or something in the church, for the priest did not reappear immediately. If all had been well inside the church, surely he would have come out and reported back. The minutes ticked slowly by. What could be going on? Still, they had an agreed plan and Alec would stick to it. Only when the thirty minutes were up did he know that he had to do something. He did not have a weapon. It had been agreed back in London that weapons would be more trouble than they would be worth. It was not worth the risk of being found with one, though the Embassy could undoubtedly have supplied him with something had it been necessary; there was always an emergency armoury and a military attaché who knew how these things worked at every embassy but it was years since Alec had needed to use a gun and he was well out of practice. And with so many military checkpoints in Khartoum, it would have been difficult to keep weaponry concealed. He decided that it was best to leave Gamal with the vehicle and strict instructions that if he was not back in another thirty minutes he should try and get Donald or David on the cell phone and ask for their help. Failing that he should drive straight back to the British Council and let them know where he was and what had happened.

He was just about to leave the truck when he remembered his rucksack. The disguise might help. He quickly got out his Arab gear and put it on over his other clothes in the back of the bus with Gamal keeping an open eye while he did so. The *jellabiya* was far too clean for someone out in the desert, neatly washed and pressed as it had been by Albert, so he had Gamal throw dust and dirt at him to help with the impression that he lived or worked in the camps. He took off his heavy boots and put on his slippers. There were not many in people in Arab dress this far out in the camps, but there were some and he would look a lot less conspicuous than if he was in his western clothes. Alec rehearsed some Arabic in his head, so that phrases were on his tongue should he need them, and then with a last few words to Gamal, shuffled through the dust towards the church.

The sun was merciless overhead at this time in the afternoon and that made it easy to move slowly, like an old Arab, across the empty space to the church. He went cautiously, mumbling to himself in Arabic as he went, and turning over in his mind the possibilities ahead of him as he played with the prayer beads in his right hand. There did not seem to be many options, certainly not as many as there were beads. Their suspicions about the church must have been well founded or Father Frankie would have reappeared. Whatever plot was being hatched, whatever it was that he had been sent to Khartoum to subvert, was being hatched in the building in front of him, of that he was certain. Alec's mind was racing, trying to think of every possibility as he slowly shuffled along. What was being planned and what could be done about it by just himself and an Arab driver? A terrorist atrocity against the West seemed most likely and that was what everyone suspected. Perhaps an Embassy bombing like the ones in the neighbouring countries of Somalia and Kenya? Somalia had never recovered from America's failed attempts at revenge in Mogadishu. But what else could it be? The British Airways plane maybe that he had arrived on? Whatever was being planned was expected to be on a spectacular scale, but what could it be? He would soon find out.

Alec did not head directly for the church. There was a shack of some sort further off in the distance and he headed towards it in the hope that anyone watching him would think it his destination. He glanced at the church every so often to see whether there was an alternative to the front door. There were no windows, at least not at eye level, and just as Father Frankie had said there were no gaps between the walls and the flat roof of wood and corrugated iron. One end of the church had the simple wooden door that Alec had seen the priest enter. He glanced at it but walked past along the length of the building to the other end. What he saw there surprised him. Large double doors that appeared firmly closed, big enough to get a truck in and out (maybe something even larger, a small plane perhaps to crash into a British Airways Boeing) and striking enough to arouse his suspicions even more. There was nothing more to see though. He threw caution to the wind and moved close to the building as if seeking some shade from the sun. He listened hard, eventually putting his ear to the wall, but heard nothing. For a moment he thought of calling out to Father Frankie but then thought better of it. There was only one course of action left. He had to find a way to see inside.

He decided to attempt it at the other end from the door the priest had used. There was nothing to be seen through the double doors, no holes for anyone passing by to peer through. He looked up and saw his chance. At the top of the doors, out of sight of anyone passing by, was a gap between the doors and the roof, quite large enough to offer a view inside if he could reach it. There was no purchase on the walls but there were battens across the doors. If he was lucky he would be able to climb up that way and look into the building, perhaps even squeeze through. Alec listened again at the wall but could hear nothing. It was eerily quiet. He grasped onto the battens on one of the doors and clambered up until he was able to put his weight on the lintel running across the top of the doors and try to peer in through the gap below the roof. Just as he was pulling himself the final few inches, the slipper on his left foot became loose and he lost his footing. The next moment he found himself falling forwards, headfirst into the darkness.

CHAPTER FIVE

Omdurman

Kati woke early to the sound of the call to prayer. It was dawn and she listened to the *mujezini* calling the faithful to prayer from the minarets close by. The city was awake and busy. People were already up and working before the heat of the day took hold. Khartoum was a city of late nights and early mornings. The diners at the restaurant last night would have stayed on eating into the early hours. The night was not for sleeping. The low temperatures were too precious to be wasted on sleep. That was something for the afternoons when the sun was high, the air was dry and it was too hot to do anything except sweat and doze.

She liked to be woken this way, her eyes closed as she listened to the sounds outside. It allowed her to place herself in this world, so far and so different from home, before she even opened her eyes. Only when the *mujezini* had stopped did she open her eyes and breathe in the morning. Already she was excited at the prospect of a whole day in Khartoum before having to return to London. She was meant to rest of course. That was what the rest of the crew would be doing; that and sleeping off their hangovers. They had looked pretty wrecked when she left them in the bar last night and no doubt another bottle of duty free Jack Daniels had been downed before they had finally called it a night. They would need their rest, before being at the airport at three in the morning for the early flight out. She would worry about rest when she was back in London.

She quickly showered and dressed. With less than twenty-four hours before having to be back at the airport she did not want to waste a minute. The next day she would be tired on the flight but that was the least of her concerns now. She did this job to be in places like this and was not going to waste a minute of the time that she had. She went down for breakfast and there were already a few people tucking into their eggs, American NGO workers at one table and a couple of Chinese at another. A woman was sitting on her own in a corner, her eyes glued to a bible open on the table in front of her. Kati's heart stopped for a moment as she recognised her as the woman on the plane who had condemned her to eternal damnation. Not wanting to be damned again, Kati avoided her eye and decided to take her breakfast away with her. She had asked Andreas to organise a car, so she poured herself a cup of coffee, took a slice of toast and a triangle of Laughing Cow cheese and went downstairs to find it. She had asked for a car, but there was a battered white Toyota pickup standing outside for her. She was hardly going to complain and guessed that Andreas had done it as a treat. He knew her tastes (as he uncannily knew the tastes of every guest) and this was going to be more fun and certainly more reliable than some clapped out Corolla that had started life in Cairo. These Toyota trucks were the workhorse of Africa and said to be indestructible.

She had no real plan but wanted to go out to the place she had done her volunteer work with Trans World Aid and meet up the children if they were still there and with Charlie who had been her best friend and so important a part of her life back then. She had tried to keep up a correspondence over the last year but it had not been easy. E-mails were impossible and snail mail was often intercepted, read or destroyed. Still, she had the luxury of a full free day and was pretty confident she would remember the way through the camps, and if she was lucky she might even get to see the wrestlers at the end of the day. All these thoughts were in Kati's head as she set off that morning. The Toyota was full of fuel which was a reassuring start and Andreas had even organised two cans of spare petrol in the back. It would not do to run out of fuel in the middle of the camps, or even worse, out in the desert.

The camps were much bigger now than when she had worked in them teaching English and basic numeracy and literacy skills, but she felt sure she could still navigate her way around them. This was her first time back since the flights had started again after a year's hiatus and she was longing to see old friends, especially Charlie. She had not said she was coming, partly because she was never sure till the last minute of her flight postings and did not want to disappoint anyone, partly because communications were so unpredictable, and perhaps most of all because she liked the element of surprise and the thought of so many astonished faces when she turned up at the church school.

It would be a good day out and she would come with gifts. She had two big boxes full of airline meals left over from the plane. It broke her heart to see the unused food binned after flights. There were always meals left over – some people who simply did not want a meal (and who could blame them?) others who fussed over what they wanted, and vegetarians who had not let the airline know of their preferences. So planes would fly into some of the poorest places on the planet, where children were dying of hunger and malnutrition, with food on board that no-one on board wanted to eat. Part of her job as she tidied up the galley and filled in the stock taking forms was to junk the uneaten meals. It was the one bit of the job that Kati could not stand, especially here in Khartoum where she knew first hand how merciless the hunger in the camps could be. So yesterday she had simply refused to do it and told the others to turn a blind eye as she stuffed the unused meals in a collapsible bag she had bought especially for the job. Warmed up on a metal plate over a little camp fire they would be manna from heaven later in the day. She even had a box of snack packets of pretzels that she knew the children would love, and she had bought a crate of bottled water from Andreas to give out along with the meals.

The last thing she needed was to be caught at a military checkpoint. All her paper work was in order and Andreas had arranged the necessary permits for the car, for her camera, and for travelling outside the city centre – endless pieces of paper all with her photograph on and all tallying with the elaborate stamps in her passport. Andreas took photocopies of them all, including her passport, and lodged them in the hotel safe. Everything should be fine, but you could never be too sure in Sudan, where the combination of the military and bureaucracy could bring any activity to a halt before it had even started.

She dressed carefully for the trip, wanting to be as inconspicuous as possible, putting on an old pair of blue jeans, sneakers, and a faded and baggy khaki shirt that hid her curves, tied her hair tightly back and pulled on a battered old hat that her father had once worn and that she took for sentimental reasons with her on all her trips. The hat was practical too. It was not wise to venture out into the sun without a head covering of some sort and the wider the brim the better. She would not pass for a man maybe, but with legs and arms covered, her full breasts lost in the baggy shirt, and her blonde hair hidden up in the hat, she would draw as little attention to herself as possible. The Toyota would help. Andreas assured her that it was as reliable as any car in the city with a serviced engine and new tyres deflated for the heat. There was also a good spare wheel and some tools in case the worst happened. But it looked knackered, battered, rusting at the edges and covered in mud and dust. No-one would give it a second glance even in the heart of the Displaced Persons Camps.

If all went well she could spend the day at the school with Charlie and her ex-colleagues and some of the children she used to teach. Then if time allowed on her way back she would drive to the outskirts of the camps and try and find the wrestlers whose picture sat in a frame on her desk back at home.

As she packed the last of her stuff into the Toyota and got ready to leave, another Toyota drove up and parked next to her. It had the word 'PRESS' stuck onto its sides, the letters crudely picked out in black tape. A camera crew emerged with seemingly endless aluminium boxes of equipment, a rather bossy woman with an English accent shouting imperious orders to her male companions. It was time to go, thought Kati, and set off jumping the first few yards down the street as she got used to the ancient clutch and nearly knocking over someone who looked as if he should be on his way to a rock festival rather than wandering the streets of Khartoum.

She set off with a clear idea of where she was going, but it took her a while to become familiar again with the streets of Khartoum and with the nose-to-tail traffic that seemed to fill the city out of nowhere during the busy hours between calls to prayer. Khartoum had a very structured day and everyone tried to cram as much as they could into the brief hours when Islam and the sun allowed them to work. As she got close to the bridge that would take her over the Nile, a taxi tried to overtake her and then swerved to a stop as its tyre burst, shedding black rubber across the road. She put her foot down and sped ahead, not wanting to get caught in the inevitable delay that these incidents caused, the thin, worn tyres of the taxis always dying in this spectacular way as they expanded on the heat of the sticky tarmac. She remembered how common such tyre bursts were on these hot, potholed roads and was glad Andreas had ensured she had a spare.

Once she hit the outskirts of town the traffic thinned dramatically and she was able take in the surroundings. There were water flagons at the side of the road put out by owners of the large, pleasant suburban houses to provide refreshment for passers by. Out of the city and within the camps themselves there was no such luxury and little other traffic, just the young Arab water sellers, children really, sat on oil drums full of water pulled along by donkey carts, dispensing their most valuable commodity to anyone who had the money to buy a cup. It was another African irony. Here she was, half an hour's drive from the confluence of the White and Blue Niles where they joined to make the world's greatest river, and yet there was so little water for these people to drink.

Kati had always had a good sense of direction, and she needed it today. It was a year since she had been to Khartoum and things had changed. Some of the camps were now virtual villages since she was last here, with modest infrastructures built up, shops of sorts as people traded goods out of their homes, and a few battered cars fought their way through the narrow gaps between dwellings. She marvelled at the way in which people could make the best out of virtually nothing, and how it was possible not just to survive but to make a life and a home in the most desperate of circumstances. The earth was baked into rutted furrows which made driving treacherous for much of the time; in the rains it would be impossible as what now were torturous roads would become rivers of red mud, water a blessing and a curse.

She was headed for one of the remoter of the Displaced Persons Camps and as she drove the density of the population thinned out, the roads becoming just wide flat spaces between houses and what had been a claustrophobic crazy labyrinth transforming into an open airy maze dazzling in the sunshine. It was a longish drive through Omdurman to Square 42, a cross between a squatter camp and a township extension, some of the dwellings tied together out of sticks and cardboard, others more sturdily built out of mud bricks. Beyond it was the desert, with mountains hazily visible on the horizon.

She made a couple of wrong turns and realised she had passed the same little cluster of buildings twice, before correcting herself and navigating through the narrow warrens of streets until she came to a large open space. It was like a village square or market place. There was a water pump in one corner, fenced in with a makeshift contraption of wood and metal and with a heavy padlock. There were a handful of communal buildings all of the same red brown colour of the rest of the buildings in the camps, fashioned out of bricks made from the clay of the Nile river banks. One of the buildings was bigger than the others and dominated the square. A little telltale wooden cross on one end of the roof indicated what made it special. It was a church. There were many throughout the camps, focal points for communal activity. She knew this church well and a feeling of deep joy flooded through her as she saw it. It had been the centre of her life while she lived and worked in Khartoum. Kati had never had much time for religion. Her parents were social anglicans and she had grown into adulthood with little conviction one way or the other. She supposed she was an agnostic if she was anything; certainly not a Christian. But when the chance to work for Trans World Aid came up she took it without a second thought. The organisation was Christian but in the quietest possible way, leading by example and not at all evangelical. Certainly nothing like the missionaries of old who came with a zeal to convert the natives. The charity was simply focussed on doing good in those parts of the world where it was needed most and where few other organisations would venture. Africa took up a lot of their time. Church was a central part of life in the camps and there were churches everywhere. The phrase Displaced Persons Camps did not do justice to the complexities of communities that were living there. This was a complex network of villages built around tribes, clans, geographical, and social groupings. Each had a church at its centre, a building that was a place of worship, of education, of social and family gathering, and the services were as varied as one would expect in Africa, reflecting the cultures, music and song that those living there had bought with them from their homes hundreds of miles away in the lush wet south of the country. Whilst she had lived in Khartoum, Kati had taken part in the life of the church in the way so many had. She avoided the long services on a Sunday morning, usually finding an excuse to absent herself from the seemingly endless singing and praise of a Lord whose love of Africa she found difficult to recognize in the poverty she saw around her.

For the black Africans from the south of the country in the camps, the Christian churches – Catholic, Methodist or whatever they were – were the institutions that made life cohesive. And not just because of the religion. The churches were cultural centres where the songs and dances of traditional and tribal groupings would be remembered and shared and passed on to new generations who had been born and brought up in the camps and had no memory of life back 'home' in the south.

It was midday now and impossible to find any shade in which to park, but she knew which way the sun was moving and drove up close to the side of the church so as to catch the afternoon shade as soon as the sun began to drop in the sky. She would be glad of that when she got back into the car later. The square was baked solid, the earth cracked so that she could have slid her fingers deep into it. No-one was about. Not because everyone was at prayer, for the most part the faith and timetables of Islam did not hold sway in the camps, but because it was too hot now in the middle of the day for anything to be done in the open.

She parked up, locked the car, though knew it was as safe here as anywhere in the world, and made her way into the church. For a moment she could see nothing. The glare of the sun outside had tightened her pupils so that the interior seemed pitch black at first. But slowly her eyes adjusted and she made out the wooden beams, the painted and simply decorated walls, the benches and tables set out for instruction.

There was a blackboard leaning against the wall. She remembered having spent much time writing on it, with a few precious sticks of chalk.

Kati went to small room at the back of the church behind the table that served as altar, meeting place for tribal elders, workbench and whatever else was required of it.

'Hello Charlie!' she said.

'Kati!' a delighted voice shouted back.

Charlotte Norton was shorter than Kati but quietly elegant, beautiful in fact, her dark hair pulled back, her blue jeans tight across her bottom, her crisp cotton shirt much more fitted than Kati's baggy number, and a cotton scarf tucked into the collar to keep the sun from her neck. She leapt for joy to see Kati after all this time.

'It's so fantastic to see you Kati. What on earth are you doing here and why didn't you let us know you were coming? We've missed you. Are you staying for long?' The questions tumbled out of her. They had both arrived in Khartoum together as volunteers and when Kati went back at the end of her time, Charlotte had stayed on, absorbed in the African life and in love with a Norwegian aid worker. The Norwegian had returned to Stavanger and a wife he had never told her about and Charlotte had lost herself in her work and the children, healing her heart with good deeds and a sense of belonging that she had never had before. She was the antithesis of Kati to look at, shorter and plumper, with a mass of dark hair that rarely saw a brush and the ruddy complexion of someone whose life was spent in the sun.

Charlotte lit a little gas stove in the corner of the room and began to make a pot of tea while Kati looked around the room and became lost in memories. Nothing seemed to have changed. Her time here had been the happiest of her life and it would have taken very little to have persuaded her to stay on again. She felt comfortable and at home, and remembered the quiet joy of simple things, when looking after the children and teaching them to read and write made her days worthwhile, and fierce friendships, conversations, and absorption in another world filled the evenings. Kati had a moment of regret that she had left it all behind, but the moment was fleeting and as she turned back to look at Charlotte who was pouring the tea into battered plastic beakers, she recognised that her need for adventure would mean she would never settle down anywhere, even somewhere she loved as much as this.

'So, tell me everything!' they asked each other simultaneously.

They both delighted in the conversation, the simple pleasure of having someone to talk with who understood. For Charlotte, someone who understood what the life was like that she had left behind; however comfortable and 'at home' she felt here in Khartoum, there was another real home that she had left far away. For Kati, someone who understood the gut wrenching pull of Africa that never let you go; something that none of her colleagues at the airline ever felt, with their need always wanting to return, never wanting to be far away from the comforts of home.

'Are you happy?'

'Yes, I think I am...' Kati hesitated in her reply because it was not something she ever thought about, enjoying as she did every moment and living for the next adventure. 'I really do think I am. Happy and lucky, I guess. What about you, Charlie?'

'Most of the time, I am.'

'Doesn't the poverty and hopelessness get to you sometimes?'

'Of course it does and if it really gets me down I take a Valium or two and just sleep it off. I do so love it here, Kati, and you know how it is – cosy in a funny sort of way, and there are a few of us who will probably be here till we die.'

'Will you never come home?'

'This is my home now Kati. I can't imagine what it must be like back in London. The furthest I get now is down to Nairobi once a year while my visa is renewed.'

'And men?'

'Oh, the usual. Hardly any and the few who do turn up aren't worth fighting over, though I can tell you plenty of us do; wet Canadians and earnest Norwegians and loads of Chinamen who keep themselves to themselves. I'm not like you. I can't just hook up with anybody. Are you still seeing that pilot?'

Kati told her about Geoff but kept the truth of Atif and her other assignations to herself. It was not that she did not want to talk about it but Atif was too big a secret to spill over a cup of tea. Maybe she felt some guilt at her secret life, or maybe it was the secrecy that kept it alive.

The conversation was getting far too deep and Kati was keen to deflect any further talk about her love life. She fished into her bag for some gifts. Some had bought some small packets of chalk, a box of pencils and a pile of exercise books, all items that she knew would be useful. She asked how things had changed since she was there last.

'It's getting better now the fighting is over in the south and some people are even going home. There's a boat going up the White Nile taking hundreds at a time back to Juba, but it's a scary journey. A German woman is running it, God knows how. The rainy season will be starting soon and they'll have to suspend the boat trips and just keep to the land convoys but I reckon they're even scarier than the river. At least you don't get lions jumping onto the boat. One of the families from here went back a month ago and a boy got dragged off by a lion while he was having a pee during an overnight stop.'

'So are there fewer people in the camps then?' asked Kati.

'If only! There are millions here and if a few hundred of the southerners go home many more refugees are arriving from Darfur and the West. It seems to be never ending.'

Charlotte made more tea as she talked. 'We've started a theatre group, you must stay and see them. Have you got time? What are your plans?'

Kati admitted she had no proper plans. She had wanted to see Charlotte more than anything and see the young people they had worked with. There was also her other rather far fetched hope which she shared with her friend – to see the wrestlers from the Nuba mountains.

'You must be mad!' was Charlotte's immediate response. 'But then you always were Kati. Let's ask around. I've heard talk of it and someone is bound to know something. You can come out with us for the day and see our shows. We are bound to find someone who knows where to find the wrestlers. Only you could come all the way to Sudan to see naked men wrestling!'

'I don't suppose they are naked these days, do you?'

'Well let me know if you find them.'

They were interrupted by young people beginning to arrive at the church. Kati knew most of them and they were as delighted as Charlotte had been to see her. There were hugs and kisses and lots of showing off of newly learnt English. Juba Arabic was often the *lingua franca* through the camps – like kitchen Dutch or Afrikaans in South Africa, because the diversity of African languages was so wide and the government insisted on Arabic. This simple pidgin Arabic had developed as a common way for people to communicate, though for no-one in the camps was it their first language. Speaking English was a sign of sophistication and education and everyone wanted to impress Kati with how much they had learnt while she had been away. A rusting hulk of a bus drove up and the kids began loading it with all they needed to give their performances: an ancient generator, spare fuel, boxes of costumes and props, drums made of battered oil cans, and the parts to make up a giant marimba. Kati helped out as the older boys clambered on the roof of the bus, tying down the bigger pieces of equipment.

She remembered Derik the driver, a huge man, black as a cell phone, with the biggest laugh and the broadest smile she had ever seen. As the last preparations were being made, Kati asked him if he had heard anything of the wrestling. He had heard things, he said. The Nuba were relative newcomers to the camps and lived on the outer edges. The authorities had banned the wrestling because it drew such large crowds. It still went on, he thought, though in great secrecy in case the military arrived and dragged people off. He thought she had a good chance of seeing it if she headed for the edge of the Nuba camp towards the end of the day.

'There are two young Nubas in the group. We'll be over towards where they live later. They will point you in the right direction.'

Tempting though it was to travel with the others in the bus, she decided to take her truck, partly because she did not think it safe to just leave it in the sun for the day, and partly because it would give her the freedom to take off on her own later should she want to.

'I'll hop in with you,' said Charlie as they all set off in great high spirits. A small child, probably no more than seven or eight had attached herself to Kati (her big sister looked after her and was in the theatre group, Charlie told her) and so Kati said that she too could come along for the ride.

'Everyone seems so happy,' said Kati.

'Don't they just. There's a real sense of hope now very different from when we were first here. The focus is shifting from the past to the future now that the war in the south has come to an end and with their traditions strong, the group are looking to find ways of making new work as they and their country move forward. You'll see.'

Half an hour later they pulled up behind the bus at a large deserted space with what looked like an open air amphitheatre made of concrete – a wide open space and steps curved around one side for seating. The young people unloaded the bus and set up their equipment. The huge marimba was put together at one side of the floor, the generator was started and attached to a sound system, instruments and props were laid out at the front and then the youngsters all returned to the bus, girls first and then the boys, to change into their costumes. Once everyone was ready the group disappeared amongst the houses and shacks and for a minute or two Kati wondered where they had gone.

'Just be patient, they'll be back,' Charlie told her.

Then she heard them, singing and chanting in the distance, the sound getting ever louder until they all burst into the performance area with a crowd of onlookers that they had gathered with them.

Eventually everyone settled and the performance began a short play about the scourge of AIDS starting things off. It was clear, witty, very funny and beautifully staged and Kati loved it. The audience whooped with joy, laughter and recognition. The generator had kept power for the sound system going for a while but it gave up half way through the twenty minute play and so the dancing and singing which needed no sound system began as soon as the play was over. The repertoire covered a wide range of traditional songs and dances from southern Sudan and the Nuba mountains. Their themes varied from love, harvest, pride, war and peace-making to social teachings and positive criticism. One song had obvious resonance and was taken up by the audience.

'What's this one about?' Kati asked.

'It's in Baai, a song from the Dinka tribe of Bahr El Ghazal State in the southern Sudan. It means 'Oh my land, you have been stolen'.'

Kati understood why it meant so much. Many of the dances would, she knew, in their home environment, have involved the naked performers whiting up their faces and bodies with flour. But there was no flour today, and no nudity, an unthinkable thing in the northern Islamic world. Instead the young performers, in their teens and early twenties, wore tee shirts for modesty's sake.

Kati knew that the Arabization of the country in recent years was a major political issue. Unlike the drama, which had been in Juba Arabic, the songs were in native tongues, vernaculars, and the sense of delight and recognition was palpable amongst the lively audience. Ancient songs took on contemporary political overtones, and old ones of love and courtship gleamed as new. There were songs and dances of many tribes, given with huge energy and commitment (no mean feat in temperatures of 45 degrees) by nearly fifty performers. At dances that they knew and loved people would come from the audience to join in, to compete, and with the older women, to show how it *should* be done.

At end of the performance Kati expressed her delight to her friend. 'Congratulations Charlie. It's just amazing what you've done with them. They're so good.'

'Oh, they did most of it themselves,' Charlotte replied modestly.

'Don't be silly, Charlie, they couldn't have done any of it without you.'

As the group were packing up after the performance, Kati and Charlotte asked the two Nuba teenagers in the group about the wrestling. They were cautious at first but eventually were persuaded to talk. 'The government have banned wrestling but if you really want to see them we can show you where they will be.'

She wanted to see the wrestling more than anything else. Charlie asked more questions and found out that the wrestling spot was not too far from where the group would be giving their afternoon performance. She talked to Derik the driver and arranged for the Nuba performers to give him directions to the site. They would stop there on the way to the next performance so that Kati would know where to go later. Meanwhile everything had been packed back into the bus and they were off once more.

Eventually they came to the edge of the camps, where the desert proper began, and the bus stopped. This was the spot the youngsters assured her that the wrestling would take place. 'Nothing will happen till the sun starts to set,' they told her.

'Come back later,' Charlotte told her, 'you'll find the way. Stick with us for the afternoon.'

It seemed like the best plan and the journey to the next stop was just a fifteen minute drive in a fairly straight line from where they were. Kati was sure she would find her way back on her own.

They had reached a place called Mayo, an area on the very edge of the camps that had not been here when Kati last visited. They had stopped this time at a large mud and straw building, another church. It was time for lunch and the food boxes and water bottles were brought out. Kati climbed onto the top of the bus to help unload the equipment while Charlotte organised lunch. She looked around her. No-one knew how many were displaced, but Kati had heard that something like three million people lived in these camps around the city. They seemed to stretch forever across the flat landscape, a labyrinth of little dwellings built of sticks and mud, cardboard and cloth: whatever materials were to hand. Thousands upon thousands stretched into the distance in an endless vista, grey and dusty in the exhausting afternoon sun which had taken the heat to over fifty degrees.

A wave of nausea and dizziness came over her and she thought she might fall off the bus. She had left her hat in the truck and the heat had got to her. Carefully she climbed down, retrieved her hat and sat in the truck sipping on a bottle of water. It would not do to get heat stroke today and she was cross with herself for being so silly as to stand in the afternoon heat with no water and no protection on her head.

The group had got ready inside the church and she watched

them coming out in their traditional costumes, plus tee shirts, dancing around the neighbourhood to let people know there was a show on. Pied Piper-like they again brought a crowd back with them and a semi-circle formed around the dancers, three middle-aged women from the audience joining the young performers the moment things began.

'The different tribes struggle to keep their customs, traditions and cultures alive here just as they struggle to find food and water,' Charlie explained. 'Now that there is a possibility of return it's all the more important to help them hold on to their cultures to be able integrate when they get back home.'

'Where do they learn the songs?'

'The dances are learnt from within the group and from teachers brought in. Often at a performance a woman will complain that there was no dance from her tribe. "Then you must teach us one," we tell her, and she is brought in to the church one afternoon to do just that.'

The Kuku, Acholi and Lokoya from Eastern Equatoria, the Dinka and Jur Chol from El Ghazal, the Shilluk and Anywak from Upper Nile, the Bari of Juba, the Zande from Western Equatoria and the Kwalib from the Nuba mountains of Kordofan, all found their songs and dances alive in the repertoire of Charlotte Norton's little theatre troupe. After the singing came another drama called 'The Well'. A couple wearily drew the last water from a deep well and shared it out. Then by a miracle the well sprang with water. Everyone could drink. A soldier came by on a bike and stopped the celebrations. He pissed into the water and then shot dead those who protested. The others took their revenge by strangling him with the rope that drew the water from the well. All was beautifully staged, with no words; only drums and the homemade marimba providing a soundtrack and the dust from the ground as make-up. The audience giggled and roared with recognition and appreciation.

It had all been unbearably hot when things began, but as the shadows lengthened and a warm breeze came in from the desert, the temperature began to drop. The stomping dances kicked up a storm of dust as the sun and the temperature began to go down. The day was coming towards a close and the dancers became shapes and noises in the gloaming, lost in dust and in the shadow of the church as the sun began to slide behind it.

It was time to go. The bus was packed in an instant and the group got ready to return to base. The young performers were in high spirits, playing 'song wars' on the way home in the dark – each end of the bus vying with the other as to which could sing most loudly and most expressively. Kati gave Charlotte a big hug and, promising to keep in touch, went off to find the wrestlers of whom she had dreamt so much. It was not until she was well on the way that she realised Charlotte had left her scarf on the seat next to her. Perhaps she could ask Andreas to find a way to return it.

Though she felt pretty confident of where she was going, Kati got a little disorientated for a minute or two and wondered if she was lost.

'How can I be lost if there are people I can ask for directions?' she reassured herself.

It was getting late and the shadows were getting long, longer than she would have thought possible, one building casting its shade for yards and yards across the red earth as the sun went down behind it. She was now at the far edge of the camps. Ahead was the desert and the setting sun.

As if out of nowhere she came upon a stream of men walking to the wrestling site. She followed them to one side at a discrete distance, not sure what the cultural protocols would be and not wanting to cause any offence, however unwittingly. After a few minutes they reached their destination and found a thousand men or more in a vast circle. The women were in the background and Kati stayed with her truck further back still, clambering out to sit on the roof so as to see what was happening.

In the middle of the circle a referee was encouraging and controlling the contestants with his whistle. The objective was simple: to push your opponent to the ground. The bouts were fast and furious. As one man was pushed over the referee would call another in to take his place and challenge the victor. The crowd were really enjoying themselves in the lengthening shadows. On the flat dusty desert floor the shadows got very long, stretching from one side of the vast circle of spectators to the other, men at the front shouting and cheering, women behind more demure in their appreciation. In the hazy evening light Kati was transported, immersed in the joy, delight, pride and celebration that Leni Riefenstahl had photographed almost fifty years ago far away in the Nuba mountains from which these people had been displaced by war. She pulled her camera out of the glove compartment and stood on the roof to take some photographs. The whole scene was illegal and taking photographs of it, with an unlicensed camera, more illegal still, but she wanted to record this moment, as extraordinary as any she had experienced in all her travel. These were not the glistening, oiled bodies of the photographs she knew, these were men in torn trousers and tatty vests covered in dust, and she could not get close enough for any dramatic shots, but she joyed in just being there. Quickly she took a few snaps before anyone could notice.

She had not seen another white person, except for Charlie, all day, let alone another white woman. However discrete her dress she drew attention to herself by her gender and her colour. A few heads turned as people heard the click and whirr of her camera and Kati began to get anxious about getting back.

The wrestling was still going on but she decided it was time to make a move. The shadows were lengthening even further and it would soon be dark under the stars, with just the odd flickering candle to show that people were living out here without electricity or water. She wanted to make it back to street lighting before it was too dark. The quickest way would be to skirt the edges of the camps for a while until she came up to a tarred road. It would be the safest thing this time of day. She wanted to avoid any possibility of hitting something or someone in the dark. This was not the place to hit a sleeping camel, even driving a Toyota. She pushed the truck into gear and set off, skirting the settlements. She would be back at the hotel in an hour, could download her photos on the computer there, e-mail them to herself for safekeeping and then wash off the day in a long warm shower and get a good night's sleep ready for the flight home tomorrow.

'Are you happy?' Charlotte had asked her and Kati knew that for the moment she was.

Just as she was thinking this she was blinded by the headlights of a truck careering towards her as if out of nowhere. She swerved out of the way just in time as it sped past. Another was only moments behind. She had no time to make anything out as they raced past with no concern for her or anyone else who might be in their way. She was shocked and wondered who on earth could have been racing across the desert after dark like this. Surely only the military would be out here this late and driving so recklessly. But if it was the military why had they not stopped when they saw her and asked her questions? It all happened so quickly that she hardly got a look at the vehicles but was sure they had logos from the World Food Programme on their sides.

In her haste she had stalled the truck. The other vehicles had disappeared and Kati found herself in silence, enveloped with the great clouds of dust they had thrown up as the went by. For a while she could make out nothing as the dust swirled around her and the loudest sound seemed to be that of her heart pumping from the adrenaline that had come to her aid. She was calm though. Kati was always calm. Calmness came with her personality and it came with the training for her job. The lights had dimmed when the engine cut out but as the dust settled their beams shone far into the distance. She looked to see if she could make out where the trucks had come from. It took a while for her eyes to focus ahead. The headlights blanched out the land in front of her and for a moment or two she could see nothing but the hardened earth stretching ahead of her and the tracks of the trucks that had passed her etched in the sand.

She noticed something in the distance, a building of sorts. She put her headlights on full beam. It seemed to be a church, just like the ones she had been to earlier in the day. Perhaps it was one of those churches she had been to earlier and she had been driving around in circles. Then she noticed a flicker of light and smoke coming from the building. Something was amiss. She put the Toyota into gear and sped towards the flames.

CHAPTER SIX

Capture

Alec tumbled forward into the darkness and something soft broke his fall. He had landed on a sofa. It had been quite a drop and it took him a while to come around. As he extricated himself from the confusion of his dress and tried to sit up, his eyes focussed on the room around him. He could just make out a figure sitting on a chair in front of him, his face illuminated by the glow of a fat cigar. Other shadowy African figures were working in the background.

'Howdy,' said a voice. 'Good of you to drop in. You really should have used the front door you know; it would have been so much easier. I guess you know the big priest. We had quite a battle to tie him up, didn't we Father?'

An American voice was the last thing Alec had expected to hear and he was quite confused. Alec's Arab clothing was up around his waist and he had lost his hat somewhere in the fall.

'*Marhaban*,' he said, thinking it was at least worth a try.

'Why, *marhaban* to you too. That's quite a get-up your wearing. Let's have some lights on boys.'

One of the men pulled a cord on the generator and it jumped into life. The room was suddenly seared with light and Alec had to close his eyes and squint before he could make anything out.

Father Frankie was tied to a post at one side of the room, his hands bound behind him and his feet tied together. A piece of tape was stuck over his mouth. The American snapped his fingers at one of the Africans and he leant over and roughly pulled the tape from Father Frankie's mouth.

'Sorry, I guess the aerial was for CNN.' Alec heard the voice of Father Frankie as he felt his arms being pulled behind his back, dragging him to a chair where he was tied with course rope. Strong hands ripped open his robes revealing the shirt beneath.

'Actually I much prefer the BBC,' said the voice. 'Welcome, we've been waiting for you.'

Alec lifted his head and turned to the voice. It came from a figure slouched across an old office chair, his long legs in cowboy boots and a Stetson on his head. Whoever this might be it certainly was not the *Mahdi*. He was an imposing figure even sitting down. His skin told of years in the desert, crevassed with hot sun, the dust of the land engrained in every pore. Sunglasses obscured his eyes.

'Are you okay Father?'

'I'm fine Alec, don't worry about me.'

'Alec is it?' said the American. 'Real pleasure to meet you buddy. What brings you out here to darkest Africa? The priest I can understand but you I'm not so sure about.'

Alec was still trying to get his bearings, looking around as he pulled fruitlessly on the ropes that bound his hands behind his back. Whatever this place might have looked like from the outside, inside it was something very different; this was certainly no church. Two trucks were parked close to where he had fallen. They were white under the grime, mud and dirt that was splattered all over them, only the windscreens were clean where the wipers had cut through the red mud. What was even stranger than seeing the trucks was the sight of World Food Programme emblems stencilled on their doors. This did not look like an aid effort and no aid worker would have tied Father Frankie to a post. Beside the sofa that he had landed on were a few comfortable chairs, crates of water and a refrigerator. The small generator chugged in the corner hooked up to the two wire-caged fluorescent lights that were slung from the ceiling and provided a bleak white light to the centre of the room. At the other end was the American, stretched in front of a desk covered in maps, some papers, a couple of walkie-talkies and a radio. The three black Africans were busy in the shadows with World Food Programme sacks and cardboard boxes. They appeared to be sorting them and piling them carefully into the trucks.

'Looks like you're working for the World Food Programme,' Alec replied, not wanting to get drawn into talking about his own activities.

' "Looks like" is about right buddy, just so long as you don't look too closely. I'm just a simple trader. What line of work are you in Alec?'

Alec explained that he was here to give a talk for the British Council and that he had been out for the day with the priest on a field trip.

'Why, that don't sound any more likely than me giving out US rice to starving Africans, now does it boys?' The American's voice boomed across the room and he laughed at his own joke, his African workers looking up at each other and smiling.

Then there was silence broken only by the sound of the generator. The American got up from his chair, walked over to Alec and removed his shades. Alec saw piercing blue eyes staring down at him, what the Arabs would have called evil eyes. From the moment the infidel had first set foot in Arabia the Arabs had thought of blue eyes as the eyes of the devil and ever since, throughout the Muslim world, blue eyes, 'the evil eye', had been cast in glass and hung at every doorway to ward off outsiders. Alec was confused and wondered if the sun was playing tricks on him. Who was this guy?

'So what really brings you to Khartoum, Alec?' said the American.

'I'm here to stop you,' Alec replied, knowing he had nothing to lose.

'You really think you can?'

'Oh yes,' Alex was bluffing now but had nothing to lose. He needed something if the plot was to be foiled, needed some indication at least of what the plot actually was. Tied up and helpless though he and the priest were, he needed to take the initiative.

'We know what you are up to.' It was the most pathetic of bluffs and he sincerely hoped it would not be called.

'Do you indeed? And you think that you and an old Irish priest are going to stop me?'

'We aren't alone.'

'Really Alec, give me some credit. I may look like a dumb American but I ain't as stupid as you take me for.'

'Don't be so sure. We have the forces to stop this little *jihad* that you're involved in.'

The priest had been quiet till now.

'I don't think this is the *Mahdi* you've been looking for Alec.'

'Why you weren't thinking I was the *Mahdi* were you now? I sure as hell ain't the *Mahdi* am I boys? Some folks do call me *El Wahid*. That means 'The Only One!' Ain't that the truth boys?'

His men laughed as they continued with their work. 'I guess the folks that sent you have got their wires crossed.'

'You're not religious, then?' asked the priest.

'Religious? Me? Like I told you, I'm just a trader. Do you think I give a damn which crazy religion people believe in? Where or what they worship? Do I care that the Chinese who are drilling for oil are communists or their British conspirators are atheists? That the animists in the south cheerfully believe that God is in everything and that their ancestors come to them in their dreams and instruct them to slaughter goats and organise drunken parties? Or that you are here peddling your Catholic mumbo jumbo in the middle of Africa, Father?'

'So it's really nothing to do with religion?' Alec wanted to know, thinking that direct questions were the only way forward.

'It's not about religion Alec, or oil come to that.'

'So what is it about? You say you're a trader, what is it that you trade?'

'Whatever it is there's a market for. Minerals, people, all the things that have been traded in this blighted and beautiful continent since before anyone can remember. There have been traders here before we whites arrived and there will still be traders here long after we've gone. It was those little palm nuts that brought you English here in the first place.'

'Palm nuts?' asked Father Frankie.

'You bet. That's what the Brits and the French and Belgians were fighting over a hundred years ago. Needed them to replace the whale oil in their lamps once the whales got too expensive. And there's a good market in them again today to make bio-fuels now the Arab oil's got too expensive. I've got friends doing a good business in palm nuts.'

'I'm thinking that it's not palm nuts you've got in those bags,' said Father Frankie.

'You're right there, Father, and it ain't just rice for the World Food Programme either. It's about something far harder and more durable than either of those.'

He walked over to where the sacks were being sealed and loaded into the trucks and plunged his hand into one of them. As he lifted out his hand, amidst the rice a trickle of sparkling stones fell through his fingers.

'Diamonds,' Alec whispered.

'Too damn right it's diamonds.'

'Diamonds?' asked the priest, 'there are no diamonds in Sudan?'

'That's what makes it a great place to export them from. No-one is looking for diamonds here. But there are plenty nearby and once they are over the border they are impossible to trace. Diamonds aren't forever Alec, despite what you might have been told. The South Africans know that. Kimberley is coming to the end of its life and the diamonds there will soon be exhausted. But the demand doesn't diminish, my friends, and it's up to people like me to find the new sources the market needs. The rice is a good cover and it protects the raw diamonds from chipping on each other. It's just perfect!'

'So you aren't involved with a *jihad* against the West?' asked the priest, equally as confused now as Alec was.

'The very idea! I'm just creating mischief. I'm a businessman going about my business using the dust of war to cover my tracks. Sudan has been a no-go area for years, no guide books, no diplomats, no tourists, even the missionaries gave up on the place years ago. As long as Sudan is unstable, it's perfect for my purposes and I intend to make sure it stays unstable. In Sudan I've created the ideal place to launder African jewels, a warehouse for diamonds from West and Central Africa, coming out via Khartoum and on to through Egypt, Ethiopia and Uganda to Europe.'

'Blood diamonds,' spat Father Frankie with real contempt in his voice.

'That's rather an emotive phrase isn't it? They are no bloodier than any other precious stone. You've been watching too many movies.'

'Who the hell are you?' Alec wanted to know.

'I'm sorry, how rude of me not to introduce myself. The name's Crockett. Woody Crockett. Just a simple businessman trying to make a living in Africa.'

'Where do your diamonds come from?'

'Mostly they come in from the Central African Republic. I don't suppose you've even heard of it have you Alec? Landlocked in the very darkest heart of Africa. Every country that borders it is in a state of constant turmoil. It's the very end of the earth as far as most people are concerned. Even those who profess to be trying to save the continent with their tawdry pop songs, commissions and manifestos, have no idea where the Central African Republic is, or if they have, have despaired of it. It is the one place in the world without hope. Greed is the only creed the people there know. There's still a French consul, but even he is afraid to step outside of his enclave in Bangui, and disappears back to Paris every time there is a coup. No-one dares go out in the capital wearing jewellery, yet the diamonds that nestle in those rings and necklaces most likely came from the open cast mines just out of town.' The American smiled as he lit himself another cigar.

'Where children can do the digging for you with only their bare hands as tools?' asked Father Frankie.

'So much more economical than all that deep mining in South Africa and men having to be transported across the continent in their gumboots to work. Here we need only children and Africa has a plentiful supply of those.'

'But that is deadly work.'

'Deadly maybe, Father, but it is work and I'm the one employing them. Bringing a little employment to a place your God has forsaken many years ago. Would you have them grow up and die slowly of AIDS or die quickly where they are working? They dig the diamonds and they dig their own graves. It is a virtuous circle of production. Nothing is wasted.'

It was Alec's turn to be shocked. 'And you get away with it?'

'Nobody notices, or if they do it's too big a problem to tackle and they turn a blind eye. And you Europeans love your trinkets and baubles. What would the gem cutters of Amsterdam do if I was not supplying them with diamonds? What would your Queen wear on her head or your film stars dangle around their necks at the Hollywood Oscars?'

'Is it just about that? Can that be possible?' It was beyond the priest.

'It's a lot to do with that, but there's an industrial side to it of course. Industry depends on diamonds as much as starlets do.'

'Does nobody care?' the priest was more distraught than angry now.

'There was a little spurt of interest after 9/11 when the Americans realised that their neglect was allowing Bin Laden to fund his network with conflict diamonds from the middle of

Africa. But no-one knew how to begin to intervene. There are no diplomats there except for that poor French bugger, no aid agencies, no journalists. Who knows what is going on? Maybe I do. And a few diamond merchants who ask no questions. Once they are on the streets of Amsterdam or in the windows of Tiffany's in New York, why would anyone make a connection with what goes on in this benighted corner of the planet? In the end the western world needs its diamonds just as much as Bin Laden does. And I can supply them. We westerners depend on the Third World to fulfil most of our needs, and the more frivolous the needs the greater the poverty of those that fulfil them – it's the same with televisions assembled in China, cushions embroidered in India, exotic spices from Bangladesh.'

Alec was intrigued now and felt that the longer he could keep the conversation going the more chance they had of finding some way to escape. 'Aren't they tempted to steal?' he asked.

'Of course they are tempted, wouldn't you be? That's why we chop their hands off. Sometimes at the end of the week. Even if there's been no stealing we cut off a hand or two *pour encourager des autreurs*.'

'Aren't there laws about this sort of thing? I thought the diamond trade was closely monitored these days?'

'The 'Kimberley Process' you mean? It's hardly worth the paper trail it's written on. You think it's not possible to forge some scrap of African paper and cover it with stamps in languages you've never heard of? Don't be so naive buddy. Or perhaps you're just an innocent like all the others who have come here before you. The African sun has bleached the brains of more innocent fools than you can possibly imagine: all here with their simple solutions – Christianity, Communism, Islam, Free Trade, Good Governance, Democracy, Aid...has any of it made a dime of difference, here in the real Africa?'

Father Frankie interrupted him. 'It's no more than slavery,' he said with quiet horror in his voice.

'Maybe,' the American conceded, 'but the Africans were selling each other long before the white man came and joined them in their trade and they'll still be doing it long after the white man has given up and gone home. It's easier to buy another human being here now than it was before your Mr Wilberforce claimed he'd abolished slavery. There are plenty involved in slavery here who haven't noticed that you Europeans have abolished it. Even in those bits of this vast continent that Europeans do like – Gambia, Senegal, Dar Es Salam – where they cling to the coast on some cheap holiday, there's still slavery going on. Tourists come to buy their little slave girls and boys and instead of taking them back to work in plantations, they just keep them for a week, fuck them and then dispose of them. It's no different from they way it used to be, it's just that now everyone gets their own little bit of the slavery action. So don't come to me with your superior morality. Telling me what is right and what is wrong here in this continent that your people have exploited for years. You have no God-given right to be here.'

'And have you?' Alec asked.

'Why not? I'm not here imposing my politics like you Alec, or my religion like you Father. I'm just buying what the people here have to sell and paying them the market price.'

'Hardly a market price surely? You're not paying them what you get for the gems in Amsterdam.'

'Of course not, I'm paying what the market here will bear

and taking my profit as I sell on. It's called capitalism, surely you've both heard of it? It's what the West is trying to export to Africa. I'm just here doing it already.'

Alec realised he was completely confused. He could not pretend any longer that he knew what was going on. 'So there won't be a *jihadi* bomber?' he asked.

'Oh there'll be a bomb alright, don't you worry about that. I'm putting all my faith in Leila Kebira!' Woody laughed again and his workers smiled back at him. He was enjoying this.

'It's good to have people to talk too who are interested in this stuff. Normally I wouldn't need to interfere. Your governments take care of everything for me, they're much more skilled at causing chaos than I am. Look how successful they've been in Somalia, it's the best trade route in Africa now and your nice Foreign Secretary is paying two guys from Leicester and Leytonstone to pretend to run the country for the social security money they were being paid back in the UK. Somalia is a perfect place for me. But things are threatening to get peaceful here in Sudan and that doesn't suit the market. Once my bomb goes off, peace will be put off for another decade and the longest war in Africa will fizzle along allowing the rest of us to carry on business as usual.'

'Surely even you want an end to the war?' said Father Frankie.

'Why would I want an end to the war? That'll mean stability, borders, Americans, Coca Cola and everything else that comes with peace. My trade will be completely fucked, Father.'

'I can't see the Americans coming in,' said Alec.

'Of course they will. They're poised as soon as the moment arises. There are Coca Cola plants in Afghanistan now, just as there are across the rest of Africa. Coke waited patiently in South Africa through the apartheid years and had bottles on the streets within weeks of Mandela's release. Just as they're waiting in Cuba and here in Sudan. Peace will bring in peacekeepers, Coca Cola and an end to my free diamond trade. So I'm just putting off peace for a little longer. There's been war of one kind or another for thirty years, another decade won't make much of a difference and by then I'll be retired. I don't plan to be here for ever. There'll be no chance at all of peace after this week. A nice big bomb. The Islamists will clamp down, the Americans will panic and the African Union will pull out; they can't afford to pay the wages of their troops as it is. So no borders or patrols, just a genuine free market. You must believe in the free market Alec, you're government's one of the last that do.'

'This is madness,' said the priest.

'You'll never get away with it,' Alec told him.

'You are hardly in a position to do anything are you? And even if you were it would make no difference. The trap has been laid my friend and nothing can be done to stop it. It has the inevitability of history, and my suicide bomber will strike without any help from me. This is not the 1930s with me plunging a detonator to set off sticks of dynamite. The world has advanced a little and Hamas and the IRA have changed the way in which things are done. And we have television now as our greatest weapon. Everything can be watched around the world as it happens. Even without *Al Jazeera* I can inflame the Arab world. Think what the *Mahdi* could have achieved if he had had CNN running his communications for him and not some poor guy in bare feet with a grubby little note in his turban.

'What was it your God said, Father? "Marvel not at this: for my hour is coming!" I reckon he got it about right on this one, it's twilight's last gleaming all around. Time to go boys.'

Woody's men had finished loading the trucks and he signalled to them to open the doors. The light was fading fast outside as the doors swung open. It would not be long till it was pitch black. The trucks were driven outside, their engines idling in the rapidly chilling air. Woody Crockett grabbed a can of kerosene and sprinkled it around the room. Throwing the empty can into a corner he rolled up his maps and pushed them with his papers into a battered rucksack.

'Good to meet you two gentlemen. Time to say your prayers, Father. Sorry you've had a wasted trip, Alec,' he said as he pulled the door closed behind him. 'A pity, I would like to have heard your little talk on plant life.' He took a reel of tape from the desk and tore a couple of pieces off, pressing them roughly over the mouths of Alec and the priest before he turned to leave. As he closed the door, the American relit his cigar, puffed on it and threw the match through and onto the floor where it spluttered for a moment and then flamed in the kerosene. Alec and the priest heard the padlock click shut as the door was locked on them.

CHAPTER SEVEN

Night

Gamal had done as they had agreed. He had waited for nearly half an hour. The minutes had ticked by very slowly as he had waited, anxious to drive up to the church himself and see what was happening. The time was nearly up and it would soon be time to make a decision. Should he go back into town and summon help or should he try to do something himself? Dusk was beginning to fall and he realised that he had not said the *Salat Al-'Asr,* the late afternoon prayer. Here, as far as it was possible to get from the city, the sounds of the call to prayer had not reached him. If ever there was a time to pray this was it. Gamal took his prayer mat from the bus and after putting it in position on the ground stood and called himself to prayer. The shadows lengthened around him as he prayed. When he had finished he rolled up his mat and put it back in the bus. It really was time to make a decision.

Whatever had been agreed, Gamal knew in his heart that he could not just return to town. He had to make a reconnaissance first in the hope that there was something that he could do. Father Frankie had left his binoculars on the front seat. Gamal took them and crept away from the truck. As soon as he was at the edge of the last little dwellings, he lay on his stomach and edged slowly forward on the ground. When he had got as far as he dared, he looked through the binoculars at the church in front of him to see if he could make out any activity in the dying light. At first all looked still, then he noticed a movement to the left of the church and saw two large doors swing open and the shadows of two trucks, without their lights on, drive out. There were two Africans in the first vehicle and one African driver in the other. He waited and saw a fourth figure join them, a Westerner in boots and a big brimmed hat. Even with the binoculars it was hard to make anything out until there was a small flash and a red glow as if someone was lighting a cigarette. The Westerner closed the doors and climbed into the second truck and Gamal was suddenly blinded by two sets of headlights. With a roar the vehicles raced off, their lights cutting tracks in the sand before them. Gamal waited again. The priest and the gardener must still be inside the church but he could not be sure they were alone. It was very quiet. There were no lights or sounds coming from the little shacks behind him and nothing either from the church ahead. Then Gamal noticed another light, an orange glow from where the men had left the church, and for a moment he could not work out what it was. In another moment he knew for sure what it was as the glow turned into flames and his nose caught the unmistakable smell of fire. It was time to act.

It was dark, that sudden darkness that comes only in Africa. He jumped up and ran back to the bus, jumping in and switching on the ignition. The engine sprang to life and he drove forward, switching on the headlights to full beam as he did so. The building and the desert ahead was bleached white, flat and stark in the lights of the bus. He could see the flames beginning to lick up around the walls and stopped before he got too close. There could be anything inside the building and Gamal did not want an explosion or falling timber to reach the bus. He jumped out and ran over to the church and around to the doors that he had seen the men leave by, shouting loudly in Arabic. The doors were firmly padlocked and he could hear nothing from inside. Running to the bus he reached in and grabbed the priest's heavy stick from the back seat, the only thing that was to hand, and then ran back again to the church and tried to break through the door. But for all of its primitive outside this was a strong defensive hideout. He started shouting, in English this time, and then ran back to the bus and put his head through the window to flash the headlights. The beams shot out like beacons across the flat landscape. He shouted for help, hoping someone, anyone, would come to his aid. But no-one in the little huts nearby dared to venture out for fear of what might be happening. Gamal took a breath and thought what could be done. The sound of the fire was growing with the flames lighting up all around.

Suddenly there was another noise and shafts of light coming from the direction in which the men in trucks had driven off. Gamal turned and saw a vehicle hurtling towards him across the sand. Now he was really worried. This could not be good, most likely it was the men returning, or worse, the Sudanese army or police on patrol and looking for trouble. His heart stopped a moment as the vehicle drew up. When he saw a blonde European girl jump out he could not have been more surprised.

'You came and God brought you,' exclaimed Gamal when he saw Kati. 'Help me please,' he shouted, 'they are trapped in there and I can't get them out.' The only sound was that of the fire which was beginning to roar as it consumed the church.

'Who?' she asked him as she searched in the back of the truck for a tyre iron.

'Mr Alec and the priest.'

Kati had no time to think. All her training exercises with the airline kicked in and she knew she had to act. She took the tyre iron and tried to break the padlock but the flames around the doors were too strong for her and forced her back. There was only one thing to be done, Kati thought, and ran to her truck. She had always wondered what bull bars were for and whether they would ever be useful. Well, now she would find out.

She engaged the 4 x 4 drive, put the truck into gear and put her foot down on the accelerator as she buckled up her safety belt. A great cloud of dust swirled into the air obscuring everything even through the strong headlights of the truck and then suddenly the vehicle leapt forward hurtling through the dark and the dust towards the church. She twisted the steering wheel from side to side so as to hold traction in the sand and in a moment crashed right through the side of the building, wood and metal crashing around her. As soon as she hit the wall she pushed her foot on the break pedal and pulled the hand break on too, so hard that it almost came out of the dashboard. The engine stalled and cut out and for a moment all seemed quiet except for the sound of the flames that were too close to the truck for comfort. She started the engine again and went straight into reverse, getting far enough away from the building to be sure that the fire would not catch to the truck.

Jumping from the truck she tore in half the scarf Charlie had left on the front seat, grabbed a bottle of water from the dashboard, doused the two pieces of scarf with the water and threw one of them to the Sudanese.

'Hold it over your face so you don't breathe in the smoke,'

she shouted as she rushed into the building. This was the last place she thought she would use her airline training.

'And turn the bus lights onto the building.'

Gamal did as he was told and then ran through the flames into the building. Kati could make out his shape with two other figures, one who seemed to be a priest tied with his back to a post and the other in Arab dress tied in a chair. She ran after the Arab, the wet cloth over her face. Gamal was with the priest pulling the tape from his mouth. 'There's a knife inside my cassock,' the priest gasped and Gamal reached in to find an ancient Swiss Army knife which he used to cut the priest free. Kati left him to it and ran to the chair where the man in Arab dress was struggling to free himself. Around her the building was blazing now, a pyre of timber and cardboard revealing a structure of steel and corrugated iron beneath. She pulled the tape from his mouth and put her damp cloth to his face. There was no time to try and undo the knots so she pushed over the chair and then dragged it through the flames. The driver had cut the priest loose now and she could see the two of them staggering out, coughing and spluttering into the beams of the bus's headlights, as the building collapsed around them.

The captives were gasping for air, their mouths and lungs filling with dust and smoke, and they collapsed exhausted onto the ground. Kati left them with the driver and went back to the Toyota. She found a fresh pack of water bottles, broke them open and passed them around. The figures, blackened with ash and dust, drank deeply from the little plastic bottles.

Kati went back to the truck and switched off the lights. Gamal did the same with the bus. The four of them had just the flames of the fire to light them, Alec and the priest collapsed on the ground, Gamal and Kati standing by the vehicles staring at the flames. The building had succumbed to the fire very quickly and Kati guessed that like everything else around here it must have been bone dry which was why it had burned down so rapidly. The large poles that had held up the roof collapsed in on each other and the corrugated metal roof came crashing loudly down, joining the vast pile of embers that were swirling in the light warm wind that had sprung up. For a while nothing was said and they all slumped exhausted on the ground and stared ahead as they drank from their water bottles and watched the fire burn out.

It was the priest who broke the silence. 'Thank you my dear,' he said. 'You really are an angel of mercy. Where did you come from?'

'Where did *you* come from?' Kati wanted to know. 'What on earth are you doing tied up in a flaming church, Father? Did you give a sermon that offended the natives?'

The exchange between them had broken the ice and as the light from the fire faded they told their stories. There was nothing any of the men could do to disguise what had really happened. The truth itself seemed improbable enough as Alec told it and there seemed little point in attempting to invent an innocent explanation for such an extraordinary chain of events. As he listened to Kati tell her tale it seemed to him even more improbable than his and he wondered as she spoke how much of it could be true. Gamal was overjoyed to see Alec and the priest safely returned to him. 'I was waiting on needles and pins,' he told them, 'and then when my hope was almost lost this lady came.'

By the time the thanks and explanations had been given it was beginning to get chilly in the breeze and there was little light to see by. It was time to make some plans. What were they to do?

'We can't go back into the city tonight,' said the priest. 'It's far too dangerous. No-one drives through the camps after dark. There's a curfew and even if there wasn't it's impossible to have any sense of direction after dark and all too easy to run over a sleeping goat or camel. Even if we were to make it back into the centre there are army checkpoints everywhere and looking like this we'd be asking for trouble.'

They realised he was right. Looking at each other they really were a sorry sight, filthy, covered in ashes and dust, smelling of the fire.

'Won't people be worried?' Kati asked.

'They will be worried,' said Alec, 'but the Embassy won't do anything tonight. There's not much they could do even if they wanted to. Will Donald do anything Gamal?'

'What is there he can do Mr Alec? He will wait until tomorrow and hope you return in time for your lecture.'

Alec turned to Kati who was lost in her own thoughts. 'What about you, won't your friends be anxious?'

'There's not much I can do. I'm due back in a few hours for the flight home and I guess my colleagues will notice then.'

'Where are you staying?'

'The Parthenon.'

'No way? That's where I am too. Won't the manager be worried?'

'Andreas? No, I'm sure he is discrete enough not to alert the authorities until he really has to. He doesn't want any trouble and it won't be the first time a guest has stayed out over night.'

Despite what she told the others, Kati really was concerned. People would be worried but what could she do? What could her colleagues do? They would have to fly back and there was always one crew member more than strictly necessary on the flight just in case someone was taken ill. Maybe they'd cover for her. Maybe they would report it but she doubted it. No-one would want any trouble and they certainly would not want a plane impounded in 'bloody Khartoum' as Geoff called it. Maybe the local agent would deal with it.

'You're right,' she agreed, 'we should stay here until dawn and then make our way back. I know somewhere we can stop off and clean up so we won't look too suspicious when we get back to town.'

As she spoke, Kati went over to have a look at the Toyota but it was difficult to see much with just the light from the dying fire and the rising moon. 'Here use this,' said the priest, bringing a torch out from inside his cassock. There did not seem to be too much damage done, just some bent bull bars. That at least was one less thing to worry about.

'Food anyone?' she asked. 'I've only got the vegetarian option. They're never popular on the African flights but we carry a few just in case there is someone who doesn't want the chicken. We can even warm them up on the fire.'

It was a little miracle, Alec thought as he watched a beautiful air stewardess serving them food in the middle of the African desert. They ate everything she gave them and then cleaned themselves up with some face wipes wrapped in foil.

Once they had eaten they realised that exhaustion was taking its toll on all of them and they decided that they should get some sleep. The nights were short and they would need to get going as soon as the sun came up. With two vehicles between them it was not too difficult. Alec, Gamal and the priest had plenty of space in the bus, though Father Frankie could not stretch his long frame out no matter how much he tried. Kati took out a rug and some cushions and lay out under the stars in the back of the Toyota.

* * *

They rose with the sun. Gamal was already at prayer when Alec opened his eyes, woken by the sound of the truck's engine starting. Blearily he got out of the bus to see what was going on. Father Frankie had propped up the bonnet of the truck and turned on the engine. He was heating up a little jerry can of water over the motor and spooning coffee from his tin into plastic airline cups. Kati was up and had opened the last of her provisions, putting little pots of orange juice on trays and warming rubbery croissants next to the priest's jerry can. They picnicked in silence, each wondering where dreams ended and reality began and all thoughtful about the day ahead. Only the burnt-out remains of the church gave confirmation of the extraordinary events of the day before. The wind had got up during the night and already the ashes were being blown away into the desert sand.

After breakfast they packed everything back into the two vehicles and got ready to leave. No-one had come out of the huts around them, frightened no doubt about what might happen if they did, until a small naked boy, perhaps two years old, appeared through one of the open doorways and stared at them. There were a few pots of orange juice left and a couple of croissants. Alec put them together on a tray and took them over to where the small boy was standing, calling a greeting in Arabic and telling those in the hut not to worry. He left the tray at the door and went back to the others. 'It's time we were off,' he told them.

They decided to go to Charlotte's church school for a clean up before going back into town. Kati led the way in her Toyota and the others followed behind in the bus. Charlotte was surprised to see Kati again but even more surprised when she saw her company. She knew the priest but who were the others? Kati did the introductions.

'You don't look like a gardener,' was Charlotte's reaction. 'I was planning to come to your talk today, the British Council has put out a three line whip to all the expats.'

In all the excitement Alec had forgotten about the talk.

'What have you all been up to?' Charlotte wanted to know.

'Don't ask,' Kati told her. 'Have you got enough water to spare for us to clean up a bit before we head back?'

They made do with a small plastic bowl and a few handfuls of water. It was far too scarce a commodity out in the camps for a decent wash for them all. The men let Kati go first, out of a mixture of gallantry and gratitude, while they had a welcome cup of coffee made by one of the older children. Gamal tried to get through to Donald on the cell phone but there was no reception this far from town. After Kati had washed she told Charlotte as little as she dared. 'Don't worry, I'll tell you everything later. To be honest, I don't really know what's going on myself.'

'Will you be at Alec's talk?'

'I haven't a clue what I'm going to do. I'm stuck in Khartoum now until the next flight comes in so yes, why not. I'll meet you there and tell you everything I can.'

They hugged and both looked forward to the chance of having a proper talk later. As she was leaving Kati remembered Charlotte's scarf and retrieved the two blackened pieces from her truck. 'Sorry about that, Charlie, I'll buy you a new one in London.'

It was time to be off. They decided Kati should go first in her Toyota and get back to the hotel before anyone else. Alec would meet her there later in the day. After they had waved her off Father Frankie asked Gamal to drop him back at his church.

'Will we see you later?' Alec asked him.

'I'll come into town for your talk tonight and meanwhile find out what I can today about this fellow Crockett. Maybe someone will know something. Whatever that American has got planned we have to thwart it.' They thanked Charlotte and were soon off again for whatever adventures lay ahead, Alec stopping to pick up a few plants on their way back into town for cover for his talk later that night.

CHAPTER EIGHT

Gardeners' Question Time

The two Davids were worried. Black David was worried because he thought that he might never see his wife and family again. White David was worried because he had heard nothing from Alec for twenty-four hours. They had spent yesterday as planned travelling through the camps of Khartoum, exhausting hours that had taught them nothing. The evening had been spent back at the Pickwick Bar waiting for Alec and Gamal. There had been no response to the calls they had tried to make on the cell phones and when the bar closed they had decided to call it a night. There was nothing they could do. In the morning white David had found the other David asleep in the back of the car and asked him to take him to the Parthenon in the hope that the others had returned in the night but when they got to the hotel there was no word from them. David let his driver sit downstairs by his car while he had Andreas bring him a coffee. Now he really was worried, so much so that he had no inclination to flirt with the pretty girl who was back sending e-mails in the 'Internet Café' and scarcely noticed the tall, beautiful, dust-covered blonde who came up the stairs into the office to get the key to her room.

'Is everything alright?' Andreas asked her.

'Nothing that a shower and a sleep won't put right, Andreas,' she assured him and walked past David and up to her room. Alec was half an hour behind her.

'Where on earth have you been?' David asked, 'I was beginning to get worried.'

'We've had a bit of an adventure,' Alec told him. 'Come up to my room and I'll tell you all about it,'

As they went upstairs David asked about Gamal.

'He's just dropped me off and gone straight on to the British Council. Have you got a cigarette to spare? I ran out yesterday and I'm gasping for one.'

Alec stretched himself on the bed with a cigarette while David stood smoking by the window. Relaxing at last after the excitement of the past twenty-four hours, Alec told David everything that had happened.

'Have we got anything to go on?' David wondered. 'We know that there is definitely a plot and definitely a bomb, and we know that this crazy American is behind it, but we don't seem any nearer to being able to stop him. He must have said something to give us a clue.'

'I know, David. I've been going over it in my head again and again. The only thing I can think of is the name Leila that he mentioned. "I'm putting all my faith in Leila Kebira," he said.'

'So we'd better find this woman.'

'I guess you're right David, but now I need to get some sleep.'

They decided to regroup later for a palaver at the Embassy. It seemed the safest place. They did not want to give Andreas any trouble and they wanted to be sure that no-one could listen in to their conversations. David left Alec to rest and said he would contact the others. 'Oh, and what about the girl?' he asked Alec. 'Do you think we should have her join us?'

'Kati? She's got this involved and has missed her flight back to London. Let's get her on the team.'

'Okay, you talk to her and bring her along later.'

* * *

Kati showered and slept then called Atif to let him know she was still in Khartoum. Alec showered and tried to sleep but his mind was busy struggling to make sense of the day before. After an hour or two with everything swirling about his brain he decided to go and find Kati. She was still dozing when he knocked and it took a while for her to get up and open the door. She opened it in a long cotton dressing gown and invited Alec in. They both felt a little awkward sitting on the edge of her bed and the adventures of last night seemed far away and unbelievable now that they were back at the hotel. Alec told her of all he knew, of the talk of the *Mahdi*, of how and why he had been sent to Khartoum and how he had ended up tied to a chair in a blazing building in the desert. In return she told him of her flight to Khartoum and her time working in the camps with Charlie. As they talked they realised just how much they had in common and the conversation became easier. They were soon chatting away about their shared love of Arabic, of student life, of travel and adventure. Kati called down to reception for some hibiscus tea which they drank as they talked until it was time to get ready to meet with the others and Alec left her to get dressed.

They all regrouped at the Embassy. Kati looked fresh in a clean new dress, a vivid floral print to well below her knees, her hair washed and loose in the sun and white heels that emphasised her height. The boys scarcely recognised her from the dirty mannish figure they had spent the night with. Alec wondered which of her two outfits was the disguise. He was back in his crumpled linen suit which looked pristine in comparison to what he had been wearing the night before. His Arab gear was with Andreas being patched up and cleaned. David was dunking lumps of sugar in his coffee. The priest was not with them. He had things to do back in his endless parish but had promised to keep in touch, keep his eyes open for anything suspicious and come into town in the evening for Alec's talk.

For a while they relaxed and enjoyed the quiet and cool of the embassy with its comfortable sofas and coffee and biscuits laid out neatly on the heavy ornate coffee table. The British had a way of adapting to the culture wherever they went and there was something distinctly Sudanese about the room with its tiled floors and low furniture. It would be very different in the American Embassy, Alec mused out aloud to the others.

'Too bloody right,' agreed David. 'They just export the mid-West wherever they go. Always travelling but never leaving home, the Americans.'

Black David sat outside under the shade of a large tree. A few workers were enjoying the shade too; taking a break from whatever it was they were doing, sprawled on the ground in their blue overalls. Gamal was kneeling in the corridor outside, facing Mecca and quietly saying his midday prayers. A couple of muted televisions hung on brackets on the wall, one with BBC World News and the other with Sudanese TV carrying its live relay from the *Moulid*. 'It's already started,' said David. 'Come on Donald, we need to make a plan.'

They drank their coffee and berated the Americans for a while as they waited for Donald to join them from the British Council. He came in dripping with perspiration.

'I've been worried. Where have you been for God's sake? I've got a full house for you tonight, the last thing I need is for you to go AWOL.'

'Calm down dear boy and have a coffee,' David told him. 'He's been off on an adventure, haven't you Alec?'

'I know, I know, Gamal mentioned it,' Donald moaned.

Donald dropped onto the sofa next to David and poured himself a coffee while Alec introduced Kati.

'I don't see what use a slight blonde is going to be,' Donald remarked.

'He's not very good with women,' David explained.

'It will cool our breasts to have you with us,' said Gamal charmingly.

'She was very useful last night,' Alec told him and went on to recount the events of the night before to an increasingly incredulous Donald.

'You'll still have to do the talk tonight. It would cause too much consternation if we cancelled. All the Embassies will turn up and the Minister of Culture is supposed to be coming, so it will look really bad if you back out.'

'What about the element of surprise. Crockett thinks I'm dead; we don't want him to know I escaped do we?'

'He's got a point,' David chimed in.

'He'll have other things on his mind and I'm sure will be a thousand miles away from here by now. He is certainly not going to change his plans – and we have only the vaguest idea what his plans are anyway. Just some woman called Leila who's going to blow up the *Moulid*. You've got to get yourself ready to give your talk and we've got to find this Leila Kebira, whoever and wherever she is.'

'She's not a woman.' It was Gamal's voice. He had finished his prayers and come into the room.

'What do you mean?' they chorused.

'*Leila el-Kebira* is not a woman, it's a day, the main day of the *Moulid*. It means something like 'big night' in English.'

Alec felt rather foolish for not having realised. 'And when is it?' he asked.

'Tomorrow. It is a most wonderful celebration. Every family will be there, the entire of Khartoum,' Gamal told them.

'How stupid and ignorant we've been,' said Alec. 'Here we are in the middle of Khartoum searching for Leila as if she was some twenty-first century Mata Hari and all the time it's not a woman, it's a day.'

Gamal had come to the rescue but most of the pieces to the jigsaw were still missing.

'We thought we knew who. Now we know when but we still have no idea who or where,' said Alec.

'We've got time on our side though,' thought David, 'if it's not until tomorrow. We'll just have to search.' He glanced up to the television screen. 'So what's it going to be like tomorrow, Gamal? Is it going to be one big party?'

'Three parties, actually,' Gamal explained, 'one in each of the cities: Khartoum, Omdurman and Khartoum North.'

'We'll have to divide up and search in each,' said Alec.

'What we need is some way to all keep in touch,' added Donald.

He was right, they all agreed, but how to do it? Their first thought was to use cell phones but they had not been much use up till then. Not that that was uncommon even in the middle of the city itself according to Donald and Gamal. Sometimes the service would be withdrawn for days or even weeks. Other times just for a few hours. It was the same with e-mails and even the land lines. At the slightest sign of political uncertainty communications would be disrupted.

'And if it isn't the politics it's the technology or the heat,' Donald spluttered. 'Nothing works in this bloody country!'

'Nothing works in this whole bloody continent, Donald, but there's no point in moaning about it,' said David.

'Everything works, it just works differently and at its own pace,' said Kati trying to calm the fraying tempers but without much luck.

'Bloody romantic,' Donald retorted. He was never good when women were involved.

'Patience,' said Gamal, 'there must be a way.'

'Can I make a suggestion Mr David?' They turned and it was the other David talking. He had come in out of the heat and was sitting in a chair in the corner pulling apart an orange.

'Go ahead, David, what's the idea?'

'Taxis, Mr David.'

'Taxis, David? Do you want to tell us more?'

'They all have radios. I have my radio in my taxi. If Mr Alec and Miss Kati have taxis as well that will be three taxis, with three radios.'

White David jumped up. 'Bloody brilliant David. Three taxis, three radios, three *Moulids*.'

'It's not a bad idea,' said Alec. 'No-one is going to be monitoring taxi radios.'

'But we won't be able to talk directly to each other,' said Kati as practical as ever. 'Someone will have to be at the taxi office to relay messages.'

'Sounds like a job for you, Donald,' suggested David. 'You've got the Arabic. That and a wedge of US dollars should do the trick.'

Donald was not convinced. 'We can't run the operation out of a Khartoum taxi office, are you crazy? What am I going to do cooped up in a smelly little cab office with a lot of young Arab boys?'

'I'm sure you'll love every minute of it and I'm sure they'll enjoy your company too.' David was enjoying this. 'All you have to do is keep the lines of communication open.'

'This is bonkers!' was Donald's considered opinion.

'It may be bonkers but it might just work,' said Alec. 'If we pair up so each car has an Arab speaker in it we'll be fine.'

'But we're talking taxis not mobile phones.'

'Never mind that. And we'll be much less conspicuous as westerners with Arab taxi drivers than wandering around on our own with cell phones. You'll just have to hire a couple of taxis for the evening Donald and sweet talk your way into the taxi office. Surely that can't be difficult?'

They were all so convinced with David's plan that Donald's reservations were quashed.

Gamal was worried that they were so few. He knew from experience what the night of *Leila el-Kabira* would be like and warned them how many thousands of people would be out celebrating after dark. 'It will be as difficult as paving the sea, or like looking for one needle in three haystacks,' he said happy to have an opportunity to use the new English idiom he had learnt the day before.

'Then we need to find out more about this needle, so that we know who we are looking for and we'll need everybody we can trust to help in the search,' said Alec.

'What about Charlie?' suggested Kati.

'Charlie who?' asked Donald.

'Charlotte Norton, my friend at Trans World Aid who looked after us this morning.'

They all agreed she was a perfect idea.

'And Father Frankie?' Kati asked.

Donald thought that he might not want to be seen at such an Islamic celebration and that he would look far too conspicuous, even out of his clerical cloths. Alec seriously wondered whether he had anything else to wear. Still they could ask him later at the talk.

'I've got another suggestion,' said Kati.

'Do you know everyone in Khartoum, Miss Johnson?' Donald asked dryly.

David could not resist intervening. 'That's why slight blondes are so useful Donald, they're popular with everyone.'

'I've got an Arab friend who works for UNESCO. I'm sure he would help.'

It was a good idea, thought Gamal, because it would be another Arab face and other pairs of Arab eyes and ears.

So it was agreed. The team would be everyone in the room: Alec, Donald, Gamal, Kati and the two Davids, with Charlotte and Kati's Arab friend. Alec smiled. 'Don't you love it when a plan comes together? Donald and Gamal, you fix things up and we can all meet again tonight after my talk. We know where and when, all we need to find out now is who and get to them before they explode Crockett's bomb.'

* * *

The British Council offices were in a spotless new building a few blocks from the Parthenon, searingly white amongst the faded stucco buildings around it. There was an improvised security check outside, with a battered X-ray machine and an extremely polite Sudanese guard taking the names of the visitors and slowly writing them by hand onto his clipboard. Alec was the 'honoured guest' they had been expecting and the beautiful white woman was also treated with great deference. A young Arab man, smartly dressed in a new Western suit, greeted them. He introduced himself as Donald's assistant and, keen to show off his very precise English, showed them around. There were a few well-used computers in the entrance area with groups of young men clustered around them. There was a library to one side and it was here that Alec was to give his talk. Donald appeared from his office to greet them all and sneaked them inside for the offer of a secret tipple from bottles of gin and tonic in the bottom draw of his desk. 'I decant the gin into empty Highland Spring bottles,' he confessed, 'and just hope no visiting government official fancies a drink of Scottish mineral water. Clear spirits are always the safest option in a job like this.'

They were grateful for the offer of drinks. It had been a turbulent couple of days for them all and a few moments' relaxation were very welcome. Alec had been so absorbed with everything else that he had quite forgotten that he was going to have to give a talk, but a second gin and tonic gave him inspiration and Donald assured him that there would be so many questions that just answering them would get him through the evening. He felt confident enough in his subject to wing it, and was keen himself to ask questions of his audience about cultivation in the rock hard gardens of suburban Khartoum.

The room was already packed when Donald took them through and he beamed as he led Alec around and introduced him to the assembled guests: diplomats' wives who looked as interested in Alec for his rugged manly charms as for his horticultural expertise, a handful of young female aid workers including Charlotte, who feigned not to have met him before, a very chatty Indian businessman who was deep in conversation with Father Frankie and an old man from one of the Khartoum universities with a passion for England who had been teaching English literature all his life and longed for the chance to speak to someone about Tennyson. Alec was charm itself to them all and Kati and David helped out with the small talk. David seemed to have plenty to talk about with the young women and was delighted when Kati introduced him to Charlotte. Atif was there too, keeping himself to himself. He knew most of the people in the room but, as just a UNESCO driver, was not on their social level so found conversation uncomfortable. He was also conscious that not even Charlotte knew about his relationship with Kati and did not want to reveal anything that would embarrass either of them.

The arrival of the British Ambassador and the Sudanese Minister of Culture caused a ripple of excitement in the room. The Ambassador arrived first, a little flustered.

'Sorry I'm so late chaps, the guys at the desk back in the FCO are getting their knickers in a twist about this spot of bother and I couldn't get the minister off the phone. Still at least I've got here before the culture chappy; wouldn't do not to have been here to greet him. That would have caused another spot of bother, but they don't seem to understand any of this back home in Whitehall.'

Donald did the introductions. 'This is Mr Messiter the Ambassador. Ambassador, this is Alec Harvey.'

'Heard a lot about you Harvey; all good, nothing to worry about. Dolly, my wife, is a great fan. She's really sorry to miss you today but she's got one of her migraines. She did say to pop around tomorrow if you've got the time.'

The Minister had come in now and there were lots of formal introductions and greetings before Alec was able to take his place and begin.

The talk went well. Alec had plenty to say about his life in England, his passion for seeds, his collecting around the world and the business he had established providing exotic plants from across the globe to the gardens of England. He got quite wrapped up in what he was saying and would have kept going had Donald not drawn him to a close and invited questions. David had dozed off but Kati had listened in delight about a world that today seemed as foreign and far away as Khartoum must have done to the good people tending their gardens back in Kent. As he had expected there were plenty of questions all of which he answered with knowledge and good humour. After a while Alec heard Donald cough politely and could see him looking at his watch and so offered to answer any other questions personally while food and drink was served. Donald gave a few words of thanks and then invited the Minister of Culture to say a few words as well. The Minister was diplomacy itself. He was a poet and not a gardener, he said, and wove an elaborate metaphor about the making of gardens with words. He thanked Alec for coming all the way out to the Sudan and, with a smile on his face, described him as a cultural colonial, part of the new 'soft colonialism' that Europe was using to keep a foothold in his country. 'You may not give us dams and hydraulic power and roads like the Chinese, but you do give us your wisdom and sell us your language,' he said.

There was nervous laughter in the room.

'So thank you Mr Harvey, we do so much hope that you will visit us again.'

There were little triangular sandwiches that could have graced any village fête back home, jugs of iced juice, and big flasks of tea and coffee. Alec was swarmed by questioners while Kati chatted to Charlotte and her friends, reminiscing about old times. David stuffed himself with sandwiches, then wedged himself into Kati's little group of young women, flirting with them all in the expectation that the math was on his side and one at least would be interested in him. As he was engrossed with a couple of blondes from Norwegian People's Aid, Charlotte grabbed the moment to draw her friend to one side.

'So what on earth is going on, Kati? You've got to tell me!'

'I hardly know myself Charlie. It all seems so completely crazy. I'm sworn to secrecy but told the others that you'd join us tonight and help out.'

'Help out with what? Oh Kati, go on tell me.'

'You'll have to promise to keep it all a secret.'

'Of course.'

Kati took Charlotte to a corner of the library. 'All I know is that it's about some plot and a bomb and the *Moulid* tomorrow night.' Kati quietly told Charlotte everything she knew and of her part in the plan to try and thwart things the following night.

'Wow Kati! Only you could get mixed up in something like this. I thought the naked wrestlers would have been enough for you. Count me in!'

'Great.'

'Do you know anything about that guy David?'

'Surely you don't fancy him?' said Kati with astonishment.

'Of course not,' Charlotte blushed, 'I was just asking.'

The Minister was the first to leave and the Ambassador followed shortly after. 'Hope you're able to sort all this out,' he said as Alec walked with him out of the building. 'Let me know if there's anything we can do to help. It's probably best I don't know too much about what's going on so that I can play the innocent to London and to the powers that be here if necessary. Donald can get a message to me if needs be.' Alec thanked him and watched the Ambassador get into his car. Then he returned to the library and gave his farewells to the other guests as they began to leave, everyone anxious to shake his hand and hope that he would return soon. Perhaps he would. It would be nice to have a quieter visit after all this was over and see some of the sumptuous gardens on the banks of the Nile that he had heard so much about. Eventually everyone had left and Donald's assistant began clearing away the debris and returning the library to its proper use. He was neat and fastidious in his manner and seemed very close to Donald. Alec wondered whether there was anything between them but then thought it best not to speculate. Donald poured what he called 'proper' drinks for those that wanted them and glasses of juice for those that did not, while Alec introduced Charlotte and Father Frankie to everybody else and Kati introduced Atif. Once they were all settled with their drinks Alec went over the plan for tomorrow, the night of *Leila el-Kebira*. They would all meet up at the hotel after noon. It was the only place where such a diverse group would attract no suspicion.

'Are you up for it Father? he asked the priest.

'Well now, I'll be a bit conspicuous but why ever not? I can sit in the back of one of your taxis and keep a low profile unless I'm needed.'

It was getting late and there was still a lot to do before the sun set tomorrow and they and the American would put their plans into action. It was going to be a busy day. As Donald's assistant continued to clear up, they went their separate ways into the sultry African night.

CHAPTER NINE

The Moulid

Alec was up early for breakfast. There was only one other person in the dining room, the woman he had seen at breakfast two days before, once again sitting on her own staring intently through her spectacles at her bible as she drank her coffee. Her long, mousey hair was tied neatly back and her shirt was buttoned tightly at the wrists. Alec could just make out her long skirt under the table. There was something very old fashioned about her, as if she had stepped from Grant Wood's painting 'American Gothic' of the farming couple with a pitchfork. He wondered if she was with a group or whether she was working on her own lonely mission. Missionaries never give up, he thought and wondered what it was that drove them in their zeal to spread the word of Christ. It must have been something that in its different ways had driven Livingstone when he was the first European to search for the source of the Nile and still drove Kati's young friend with her Trans World Aid mission. He mulled over the complexities of Christian interference as he tapped on his boiled egg and wondered about the woman at the far table.

After a couple of cups of coffee he drifted down into the foyer where a few people were already slumped in the heat.

There was a girl still tapping away at one of the computers and trying to send e-mails across the world. Alec looked at her and wondered what communications could be so important that she was forever trying to send and receive them. The TV in the corner was beaming pictures of the *Moulid* across the room capturing every moment, however trivial. Nothing would happen until after evening prayers, he was sure of that, so they could afford to spend the day making preparations for whatever might lie ahead and for a swift escape afterwards if necessary. The BBC crew was back, the journalist still just as bossy and annoying as before, the cameraman as French and taciturn, and the producer pleased to have got a story. They were asking about nightlife and what to do on their last night in Khartoum to celebrate the success of their trip to film the starving and the dispossessed of Darfur. Andreas was being as charming and helpful as ever. That was why everyone used his hotel. Alec lit a cigarette as he watched the scene in front of him and thought back on the night before. He had enjoyed his little talk and meeting fellow enthusiasts. He had been given gifts of seeds which he would treasure back home and propagate with delight in the year to come. Some of the seeds he knew, others would be a surprise as they shot up next spring. He wished he could make these trips without all the adventure that seemed to come with them. Just once, he hoped, someone would ask him to give a talk because they wanted a talk, not because they wanted him to get involved in plots and espionage.

Kati had got up early too and made contact with the British Airways office in Khartoum. It was hardly an office, just one ground agent – a sort of honorary consul – operating from a desk in the Sudan Airways building. She asked him to get a message through saying that she had been struck down with a stomach bug and been nursed by an old friend at the church she had been to visit. It was close to the truth. She had missed the return flight and would have to get out on the flight that was coming in tonight. With luck it would be a different crew and she would have less explaining to do. She knew that worse things had happened and the stories of crew members who had missed their flights home were the stuff of legends. A stomach bug was nothing in comparison to the marriages, sex changes, back street abortions, and bouts of malaria that had kept others from their flights. She consoled herself with the thought that her excuse was far from improbable and with luck she would just get a bollocking for not obeying the rules about drinking bottled water and eating only at the approved hotel. Still, crew members got worse stomach bugs from the airline meals than they ever did from eating out on stopovers, and anyway life for her had moved on, far away from obeying the rules. She was not sure she knew what the rules were any more. She was caught up in a great game which she barely understood and she had very little idea who the other players were. David, Alec, Gamal. Who were these people? The breakfast room was empty by the time she had got back to the hotel and she had the place to herself. Plenty of time then to wonder about her new friends as the waiter shuffled over with a fresh pot of coffee and a newly boiled egg.

Everything seemed so improbable. Had David really travelled half way across Africa in a taxi? If he had not, then who was the taxi driver with him? Was Alec really a gardener from somewhere near Broadstairs where her father had taken her once on holiday when she was eight? Certainly his talk last night at the British Council had been convincing, though a talk on English gardens in a British Council library in the Sudan to an audience of educated Africans, immigrant Asians, a couple of Chinamen who were probably spies and a woman from Surrey, seemed no less improbable than everything else that had happened recently. As she thought back over the events of the past two days none of it made sense, least of all the fact that she now seemed to have joined a group of misfits intent on foiling some sort of bomb plot about which they knew almost nothing.

David was sleeping it all off at the Embassy. He had managed to slip back and no-one had asked any questions. The Embassy was always discrete, the British presence causing not a ripple in the country it had once ruled. If there was any trouble nowadays the place would quickly and smoothly shut up shop until things quietened down and the Ambassador and the senior staff would take a holiday in Mombasa. It was not the most demanding posting, though it could be one of the hottest, and there was still a deep seated respect, even admiration, for all things British in Khartoum despite, or perhaps because of, the Islamification of the country. The youth queuing to use the internet in the British Council library and peer at the BBC World television were testament to that. David slept through everything in a much more splendid bed than his companions in the Parthenon, in his best travelling pyjamas, made of the lightest silk and bought for him by an old girlfriend from a place on Jermyn Street. His driver David was asleep too, under a tree in the Embassy compound. White David, in a rare moment of post colonial guilt, had even arranged for him to get a phone message through to his wife via a relative back home. A very discrete message, as the lines were almost certainly monitored. Discretion was the weather word in the British Embassy.

They were to meet up in the early afternoon at the Parthenon. Father Frankie arrived early and went up to Alec's room to find him just out of the shower and putting on his newly patched and cleaned *jellabiya.*

'I've been thinking about all of this, Alec. There's something here that just doesn't ring true. Is this Crockett chappie really planning an Islamist bomb at a Muslim celebration? And even if he is, how will he manage it? Where would he find a suicide bomber?'

'I know what you mean,' Alec said. 'I've been thinking the same. It might not be too unlikely. There are lots of rival Muslim sects aren't there and some think the whole idea of a *Moulid* for The Prophet is heresy.'

'Perhaps you're right. I keep going over everything he said to us in my head trying to pick up a clue.'

'Me too. There must be something there, just like the *Leila el-Kebira* business if only we could think of it.'

The priest and the gardener went over everything Crockett had said to them while they were held captive but could not put their finger on anything significant. They sat in silence for a while, the priest on the bed, Alec by the table which had the few plants he had collected on it, soaking in glasses from the dining room downstairs.

'Wait a minute, Father, what was that stuff he said to you about God?'

' "God is with us," was it? Something about how my God was going to be useful to him and then that passage from Isaiah, "I am God, and there is no other." '

'That's it! Of course!' exclaimed Alec, but before he could explain there was a knock at the door and Kati came in.

'Hello, Father, I thought I might be the first.'

'Good to see you my dear. Alec was just about to tell me his revelation.'

'Hi Kati, yes, I've got an idea. Maybe it's not an Islamist bomb at all. Crockett talked about your God, Father and yours is a Christian God. What if it was a Christian fundamentalist bomber, wrecking havoc at The Prophet's birthday party? Muslims of every kind will be gathered together for the celebration and one bomb could easily kill believers from dozens of sects. All hell would let loose and the West would get the blame.'

'You've got it,' Kati exclaimed and suddenly it all fell into place. The woman on the plane clutching her bible. "Then you'll go to hell my dear, I'm very sorry." Her being in the hotel. It all made sense. 'We're looking for a suicide bomber, right?' Kati said to the others. 'Maybe it is a woman. It doesn't have to be a man does it?'

'Of course not,' said Alec. 'That's why we thought *Leila el-Kebira* was a woman.'

'Quick, come with me!' and with those words Kati rushed out the door, the priest and Alec following behind her. The others were waiting downstairs in the foyer but Kati ran straight past them and into Andreas's office.

'That woman, Andreas, the one with the bible, what room is she in?'

'She's just checked out this afternoon. She said she was flying home today.'

'But there isn't a flight today. At least not a British Airways one and she flew in with us. Has her room been cleaned?'

'No not yet, why?'

'Can we have the key, Andreas? It might be important.'

Andreas looked at Kati and a frown went across his face.

The absolute privacy of his guests was paramount to the long success of the hotel. Only he and his wife knew their secrets.

'I can't just let you into the rooms of other guests.'

'She's checked out, Andreas. You just said so yourself. She isn't a guest here any longer. It really is important.'

'You are right and I trust you as if you were my own daughter, Miss Kati.' He went to get the key.

The others were bewildered.

'What are you on about?' asked David.

'That woman. The one with the bible. You must have seen her at breakfast. And she was on the plane. She's the bomber!'

'Are you sure?'

'As sure as I can be. It all fits into place.'

They followed Andreas up the stairs to a small room at the back of the hotel, overlooking an enclosed courtyard draped with washing and other bits and pieces. Andreas knocked politely out of habit and opened the door. Everybody gasped. Across the wall around the mirror opposite the bed was a collage of religious texts and messages and in the middle of the little table in front of the mirror, in a golden frame, was a picture of The Sacred Heart of Jesus.

' "Vengeance is mine, I will repay, saith the Lord," ' Kati read out and looked at the others.

"NOW see that I, even I, am He, And there is no God besides Me; I kill and I make alive; I wound and I heal; Nor is there any who can deliver from My hand," were neatly inked in green pen alongside, "He that shall blaspheme against the Holy Ghost hath never forgiveness, but is in danger of eternal damnation." Another read, "All the peoples of the earth may know that the LORD is God; there is no other."

' "Look to Me, and be saved all you ends of the earth! For I am God, and there is no other," ' read David. 'Isaiah 45:22, I know that one.'

'Look at this and worry,' said Alec and read from the quote running along a sheet of paper at the top of the wall: ' "Marvel not at this: for the hour is coming, in which all that are in the graves shall hear His voice, And shall come forth; they that have done good, unto the resurrection of life; and they that have done evil, unto the resurrection of damnation." '

'Where have I heard that before?' asked the priest.

'Woody Crockett, remember. "Marvel not at this," ' he told us, ' "for my hour is coming." '

'How did he recruit her?' asked Charlotte?

'Who knows,' Alec replied. 'If we find her maybe we can ask her.'

'You've got to hand it to the bugger, it's a devilish plan,' said Father Frankie.

'You'd better get rid of all of this Andreas,' said Alec. 'We'll go downstairs and set off to find her.'

'What's her name?' Kati asked Andreas.

'Mrs Laura Jesson,' Andreas told them.

Kati understood it all now. 'So there is a *Mahdi* of sorts. All that 'chatter' you talked about, Alec, was just misinterpreted. Laura Jesson is the rightly guided one.'

'Of course!' exclaimed David. 'It's been a double bluff. It's a day and it's a woman. And it's not an Islamist bomber we're looking for it's a Christian bomber.'

'And they will have to be conspicuous,' added Alec. 'That's the whole point. They won't want to go unnoticed or the whole plot fails. It will have to be obvious.'

'What does she look like?' David wanted to know.

'I've got a photograph of her. I had a copy made of her passport photograph for her permits.'

They waited in the foyer while Andreas made them each an enlarged photocopy of the woman's passport photograph. David was staring at the television. An attractive announcer had caught his eye. The broadcast was coming from a sumptuous tent in the heart of the festivities. Alec guessed that everyone who was not at the celebrations would be watching at home. Millions, Atif assured him, quite an audience.

'Alec, what was it Crockett said about television?' the priest asked.

'The television of course, the coverage has been non-stop. Crockett's planned for her to blow herself up live on Sudanese television.'

It had been on since the *Moulid* began. So obvious that Alec had forgotten it. Whoever was going to blow themselves up was going to do it for all to see on Sudanese television. And everyone would take an instant feed, even those countries who regarded the *Moulid* as un-Islamic.

'Where are they broadcasting from?' Charlotte asked.' Does anybody know?'

'They are at the site in Omdurman,' Atif told them, 'it's the biggest of the *Moulids* and stretches right down to the river. I had to drive some UNESCO visitors there this afternoon.'

'Great!' Alec was excited now. 'So we've narrowed it down to one site and we know who we're looking for. Let's get going!'

Donald was just drawing up in one of the two taxis as they reached the street. Alec quickly filled him in on what had happened as they hurried to get themselves organised. Kati and Atif got into one taxi with Father Frankie.

David was with his driver. 'You'd better come with me,' David shouted over to Charlotte and Kati saw a smile on her friend's face as she watched her climb in to the back of the car with him. Alec got into the other taxi with Gamal.

'Jump in Donald, we'll drop you off at the taxi office on the way!'

They could see the *Moulid* well before they got there, the multitude of its coloured lights dazzled from across the river. It was a breathtaking sight. Another world, or rather lots of worlds, spread out under a myriad of electric lights, a great expanse of carnival and the end of three days of celebration. It was a night unlike any Kati had ever seen. Here in the Islamist state of the Sudan a celebration was thriving that many other Islamic states considered *haram* – forbidden. Arab Islam meets black Africa meets Blackpool, Kati thought. On the outside were stalls selling sweets for children. Dolls for the girls, soldiers on horseback for the boys, all made of solid pink sugar, the dolls with crepe paper dresses, the soldiers with cardboard swords. She thought they looked Spanish or Mexican rather than African or Arab, perhaps they were a flashback to a colonial era or even the crusades, perhaps a sugary version of the evil eye.

'The dolls are called *Aroussa al Moulid,*' Atif told her.

Some of them were huge; it would be hardly possible for a small girl to carry home a confectionary doll that was almost as large as herself. Kati thought back to the seaside holidays of her childhood when she won a giant teddy bear at the fair on the end of the pier, or in truth her father had, and she had carried it home in triumph. Whatever happened to that bear? she wondered. How was her father? she wondered too. He would be amazed to hear her tales when she got home. For all that she enjoyed her travels, she still missed seeing him and looked forward to her visits to what was, despite her nice flat in West London, the place she thought of as home. No time for those thoughts now. Behind the dazzling white neon of the sweet stalls, there was more neon with fairy lights and festoons, colour and music, so many different types of music competing to be heard, each wafting on the breeze from the Nile.

In the other taxi with Gamal and the taxi driver, all three looking like brothers out to enjoy themselves, Alec was sharing Kati's wonderment, amazed at the rich variety of Islamic life he saw around him. The celebrations were vast, stretching in every direction. Each sect had its own area as André had said, curtained off for its own celebrations. In one place was quiet prayer, in another declamatory Koranic readings. Some of the areas were devoted to real exoticism – colourful robes, feathers, headdresses, drums, whirling dances, trances, circlings. It was a sea of breathtaking, loud, colourful parties with thousands taking part, looking on or just milling about and savouring the atmosphere. It was all an eye-opener to Alec, a vision of how varied the world of Islam was, even here in this one country. He realised how little he knew of Islam now that he could see it spread before him in its many colours. There was an exuberance here, a joy, a sense of party and celebration such as he had never before seen in all his travels. There were hundreds of families, the children all clutching pink sugar dolls and knights on horseback, the parents with smiles of delight on their faces. There were horses too, and camels, adding to a scene that at times looked almost biblical.

All three cars were driving around the vast periphery of the *Moulid*, eyes desperately searching for the woman who had been staying at the hotel. Crackly messages were being exchanged between the cars through Donald at the taxi office. Atif had found the television studio, a beautiful marquee even more brightly lit than the other tents around it. Their taxi driver got as close as he was able until the crowds became too dense and he could drive no further. Kati told Donald that she and Atif would go on foot from there, leaving Father Frankie behind in the car, and they got out to make their way through the crowds towards the television tent in the hope of intercepting Mrs Laura Jesson.

The Davids and Charlotte were far away at the other side of the celebrations and had driven off the road and come to a place where children were being given rides on gloomy-eyed camels when Charlotte noticed something and pointed to a women with a rucksack slung over her shoulder disappearing into the crowd in front of them.

'Are you sure that's her?' David asked.

'Certain, look at the picture.' Charlotte thrust the crumpled photocopy at David who took the handset of the taxi radio from driver David and called through to Donald.

'We think we've seen her Donald, get hold of the others. We're just off the main road by the camel rides.'

'They're on their way around to you, they'll just be a minute,' came Alec's message back via Donald.

As soon as they heard the message Alec and Gamal told their driver where to go and he careered off the tarred road and across the sand. In a moment they saw the others ahead of them, waving and pointing in the direction the woman had gone. The priest too had got the message and ran over to Kati and Atif telling them that the woman was heading in their direction. Alec and Gamal driver swerved on the sand to avoid a large rock in front of them and one of the tyres burst, sending the taxi sliding out of control across the sand. The driver, for whom this was not a new experience, wrestled with the steering and came down through the gears and brought the car to a halt. The taxi had scarcely stopped before Alec jumped out. He knew that there was only one thing to do.

Kati was running over from the television tent with Atif and the priest behind her when she saw a sight that stopped her dead in her tracks. There, a few hundred metres in front of her, was the woman from the plane, calmly and slowly walking through the crowds as if in a trance, her bible clasped to her breast in both her hands and a large rucksack slung over her left shoulder. Behind her, galloping through and above the crowds came a camel, the people parting in front of it as if by some ancient magic, and there precariously on its single hump like Lawrence of Arabia was Alec Harvey. He looked a magnificent sight, thundering across the hardened sand, the setting sun behind him.

It was all over in a second. The woman had no time to notice Alec before he came up beside her, grabbed the bag from her shoulder and galloped on, the camel making clouds of dust with its hoofs and the crowd parting in a mixture of fear, amazement and delight. Alec urged on the camel with his feet. If this was a bomb he had to get it away from these crowds and somewhere safe as quickly as possible. Alec looked ahead and saw the Nile in front of him, silently glistening in the light of the moon and with the colours of the *Moulid* lights reflected on its slowly moving surface. He raced that way and as he neared the bank swung the bag above his head and let it go. The wide placid river exploded as the bomb hit its surface and great plume of water rose into the air and came down like unexpected rainfall, drenching the few people who had been sitting quietly on the river's banks.

Kati felt some splashes of water on her back as she grabbed the woman who was standing rooted to the spot clutching her bible after Alec had snatched her bag.

'I've got her,' she shouted back to Atif. 'Tell the others.'

It was the woman from the plane. 'If you do not believe in our Lord Jesus Christ you will be condemned to burn forever in the fires of damnation,' she had told Kati on the flight out from London. Kati had thought her to be a lonely missionary planning to convert people as missionaries had in the past. But hers had been a very different mission and masterminded somehow by this Woody Crockett that had captured Alec and the priest.

Kati held onto her tightly while she waited for the others. Suddenly she spoke. 'Islam is a false religion,' came the tight American voice that had chilled Kati on the plane. 'You don't need a dead prophet, you need a living Christ.'

Mrs Laura Jesson repeated her words until they became a mantra, getting louder on every repetition. Kati struggled to put a hand over her mouth as the others had arrived.

'Christ!' went David, 'what are we going to do with her?'

'You might need these,' said Father Frankie bringing some handcuffs from out of his cassock.

'And some of these might help too,' said Charlotte and took a small bottle of pills from her pocket. 'They're tranquilisers. They might just keep her quiet.'

The crowd had been too excited by the charging camel to notice the bomber and the group who were gathered around her.

The priest and Charlotte gently fed her some pills and gave her some whisky from David's hip flask to wash it down. She did nothing to resist and was soon sitting in a drowsy heap on the ground.

Alec was walking back leading his camel.

David was the first to congratulate him. 'Well done old boy. Bit of a risk though. What if she'd set it off?' 'She wasn't going to do that until she was at the television tent. At least that's what I hoped.'

'I'll take it from here.' They looked up and saw the unexpected figure of a new age hippy standing beside them. 'The Club sent me to pick up the pieces, I'll look after her. We don't want the Americans getting involved.'

CHAPTER TEN

Homeward Bound

They had all made their farewells at the hotel the night before and Alec saw no-one as he had a late breakfast in the morning. The flight was not until after lunch but it would take a good three hours at the airport for every little stamp and squiggle in his passport to be checked and for the luggage to be combed through three or four times before he was allowed to depart, so he planned to leave as soon as he had finished his coffee. He guessed that David had set off back to Kenya in his taxi and wondered what the meter would say we he eventually crossed back over the border. Father Frankie had gone long ago, slipping back into the vastness of his parish and keen not to be caught up in anything more. Donald would take Alec to the airport and oil the bureaucracy of departure.

Kati had been up very early and was the first to have breakfast in the hotel dining room, the elderly waiter showing no surprise to see her transformed in her British Airways uniform, smart and fresh, the skirt discretely below her knees so she would not cause offence while still in Khartoum. She had not had a chance to say goodbye to any of the others in the excitement of the previous night and wondered where they all were that morning. In the chaos and confusion there had been no plans made to see each other again and she had not even had time to say a proper goodbye to Atif. She settled up with Andreas who was sitting in his office with scraps of paper and receipts, entering figures into a large ancient ledger that had probably been in the hotel as long as he had. 'Do you ever sleep?' Kati asked.

'Once a year, back in Greece on my holidays,' came the reply.

What was it that brought him back to Khartoum when he could be living a comfortable life back in Athens she wondered.

Andreas organised a taxi for her while she went back for her bag, an old bag of her father's that that she had travelled with since she was a student and was the one possession she really treasured. It had been around the world with him on cruise ships and tramp steamers, on sea planes and transcontinental trains, and now it was travelling with her. She had one last task to do before getting to the airport. Just as her father had always bought her a gift every time he returned from his travels, so she now did the same for him. She realised now how important those souvenirs must have been to him just as they were to her, reminders of places he had been and a collection of links between the two of them, a web of travels and memories and connections that joined them together. She hugged Andreas and skipped down the wide, well worn steps to the waiting taxi and asked to be taken to the *souk* on the way to the airport to pick up something for her father.

It seemed that you could buy anything in the *souk* and despite the apparent chaos and confusion, there was a strict order to the place that Kati knew well. She had very little time and decided to get something from one of the metal workers with their wares spilling out from the dark and gloomy interiors onto the street, sparkling and catching the sunlight, a cornucopia of cooking equipment all hand-beaten with a rough practical finish ready for use rather than decoration. She stopped the taxi and stepped out, standing still for a moment to let her eyes adjust to the glare. There were hundreds of things to choose from but a little round coffee pot, with a long spout, just big enough to hold a cup of the local thick, aromatic coffee rich with the smell of cardamoms, caught her eye and she thought it the perfect thing. There was not time to haggle and the trader was as surprised to get his asking price as he was to be selling something to a tall, blonde foreign woman.

'*Shokran jazeelan*,' she thanked him.

'*Al'afw*,' he replied delighted to have been the one she had bought from as his neighbours clustered around to watch the transaction. Buying and selling in the market was too important an activity to be rushed and she regretted not being able to stay and explore deeper into the *souk* but she had to rush if she was to get to the airport early enough to not annoy her colleagues even more than she had done already.

Alec had little to pack. The seeds he wrapped in a bit of kitchen film and tucked them inside his used socks, just in case an over officious customs officer wondered what he was bringing back from the middle of Africa. He settled his bill, retrieved his passport and US dollars from the hotel safe and had a last coffee and chat with Andreas. The American girl was still tapping away at the computer in the corner. Had she been there all week?

Gamal took Alec to the airport. Donald was already there to smooth things over and help him with the paper work. The BBC team was there with a pile of equipment, the female reporter remonstrating with the officials who were surrounding them and arguing about the departure tax that they were demanding from her and her team. Her French cameraman was sitting on his camera cases silently rolling a cigarette, resigned to the irritation of both the officialdom and his reporter colleague. Alec nodded to him as he slipped past and through to the VIP lounge hoping that if they were trying to get on the same flight as him they would not hold everything up. He was ready to get home now, the flight a few hours of tedium before he could be back in London and then just a few hours more to the quietness of his home and gardens.

Donald returned with his passport for the last time and there was nothing to do but wait for an hour or so until the flight was boarding. A counter for refreshments opened and Donald bought them both cartons of juice. Then at last the call for the flight came and they took their leave of each other, rather formally shaking hands, Alec fighting an impulse to give Donald a big hug. He had come through in the end and Alec felt a surge of emotion for this man he had known for only a few days and who he was leaving in his personal limbo of closeted ex-pat life. The passengers walked to the plane across the scorching tarmac, a straggling line holding onto their hats as gusts of wind tried to snatch them from their heads, a collection of travellers very similar to the one he had flown out with. Alec stubbed out his last cigarette on the tarmac and climbed the stairs to the plane. At the top the steward took his ticket and gave him a little smile. 'To the left, sir, just take any seat in rows four or five.'

To his surprise he found that he had been upgraded. Perhaps Donald at the British Council had pulled a string.

As he turned into the first class cabin, he saw Kati standing there, transformed in her British Airways uniform, with a small tray and a glass of champagne on it. She smiled at him as he took his seat. He smiled back and accepted the drink. It was going to be a pleasant flight.